PATRICK MODIANO

PARIS NOCTURNE

TRANSLATED FROM THE FRENCH
BY PHOEBE WESTON-EVANS

TEXT PUBLISHING
MELBOURNE AUSTRALIA

textpublishing.com.au
The Text Publishing Company
Swann House
22 William Street
Melbourne Victoria 3000
Australia

First published in French in 2003, by Éditions Gallimard as *Accident nocturne*

First English publication in 2015 by The Text Publishing Company

Cover & page design by W. H. Chong
Typeset by J & M Typesetting
Printed in Australia by Griffin Press, an accredited ISO/NZS 14001:2004 Environmental Management System printer

National Library of Australia Cataloguing-in-Publication entry
Creator: Modiano, Patrick, 1945- author.
Title: Paris nocturne/by Patrick Modiano; translated by Phoebe Weston-Evans.
ISBN: 9781925240108 (paperback)
ISBN: 9781925095920 (ebook)
Subjects: Psychological fiction, French. Memory–Fiction.
Other Creators/Contributors: Weston-Evans, Phoebe, translator.
Dewey Number: 843.914

 This book is printed on paper certified against the Forest Steward-ship Council® Standards. Griffin Press holds FSC chain-of-custody certification SGS-COC-005088. FSC promotes environmentally responsible, socially beneficial and economically viable management of the world's forests.

For Douglas

LATE AT NIGHT, a long time ago, when I was about to turn twenty-one, I was crossing Place des Pyramides on my way to Place de la Concorde when a car appeared suddenly from out of the darkness. At first I thought it had just grazed me, then I felt a sharp pain from my ankle to my knee. I fell onto the pavement. But I managed to get up again. The car swerved and collided with one of the arcades surrounding the square in a shower of broken glass. The door opened and a woman stumbled out. A man who happened to be at the entrance of the hotel under the arcade ushered us into the lobby. We waited, the woman and I, on a red leather sofa while the man made a phone call from reception. She was cut along the hollow of her cheek, on her cheekbone and on her forehead, and the cuts were bleeding. A huge man with short brown hair came into the lobby and walked towards us.

Outside, they surrounded the car, which stood with its doors hanging open, and one of them took notes as if for a report. As we got into the police van, I realised that I was missing my left shoe. The woman and I were sitting side by side on the wooden bench. The huge brown-haired man sat on the bench opposite us. He was smoking and glanced at us coldly from time to time. Through the barred windows I could see that we were driving along Quai des Tuileries. I hadn't been given time to collect my shoe, and I thought about how it would stay there, all night, in the middle of the pavement. I could no longer tell whether I'd lost a shoe or an animal, the dog from my childhood that had been run over when I lived on the outskirts of Paris, Rue Docteur-Kurzenne. Everything was getting muddled in my mind. Perhaps I hit my head when I fell. I turned to the woman. I was surprised she was wearing a fur coat.

I remembered that it was winter. And the man opposite was wearing a coat, too, and I was wearing one of those old sheepskin jackets you find at flea markets. Her fur coat was certainly not one you would find at a flea market. A mink? A sable? She was smartly dressed and well groomed, which contrasted with the cuts on her face. On my jacket, just above the pockets, I noticed spots of blood. I had a large graze on my left palm; the spots of blood on the fabric must have come from there. She held herself erect but with her head tilted to one side, as if staring at something on the floor. My shoeless foot, perhaps. She had shoulder-length hair and in the light of the lobby she seemed blonde.

The police van stopped at a red light on the quay, level with Saint-Germain-l'Auxerrois. The man continued to watch us in silence, one at a time, with his cold stare. I couldn't help but feel guilty of something.

We were still stopped at the lights. The café on the corner of the quay and Place Saint-Germain-l'Auxerrois, where I had often met my father, was still open. It was time to escape. Perhaps all we had to do was ask the guy on the bench to let us go. But I felt incapable of uttering a single word. He coughed, a chesty smoker's cough, and I was startled at the sound. Since the accident, a profound silence had settled around me, as if I had lost my hearing. We continued along the quay. As the police van headed over the bridge, I felt her hand squeeze my wrist. She smiled, as if she wanted to reassure me, but I wasn't frightened at all. It even seemed to me that we had been in each other's company before, at another time, and that she still had the same smile. Where had I seen her? She reminded me of someone I had known a long time ago. The man opposite us had fallen asleep and his head had dropped onto his chest. She squeezed my wrist hard, and I was convinced that soon after, once we were out of the van, they would handcuff us to each other.

After the bridge, the van went through an entrance-way and stopped in the courtyard of the Hôtel-Dieu casualty department. We sat in the waiting room, still accompanied by the man. I was beginning to wonder exactly what his job was. A policeman in charge of keeping an eye on us? But why? I wanted to ask him, but I already knew he wouldn't be able to hear me. I had LOST MY VOICE. The three words came into my mind in the stark light of the waiting room. The woman and I were sitting on a bench opposite the recep-tion desk. The man went to talk to one of the women there. I was sitting very close to her; I could feel her shoulder against mine. He sat back down in the same place on the edge of the bench, along from us. A red-haired man, barefoot, dressed in a leather jacket and pyjama trousers, paced up and down the waiting room, shouting across at the women at reception. He complained that they weren't paying him any attention. He kept walking in front of us, trying to catch my eye. But I kept my eyes averted because I was afraid he would talk to me. One of the women from reception went over to him and gently guided him towards the exit. He came back into the waiting room, but this time he launched into a tirade of complaints, like a howling dog.

From time to time, a man or a woman escorted by officers would cross the room quickly and disappear into the corridor opposite us. I wondered where the corridor led to, and if, when our turn came, we would be steered down there, too. Two women crossed the waiting room, surrounded by several police officers. I could tell that they had just come out of a police van, perhaps the same as the one that dropped us off. They were wearing fur coats, just as elegant as the one worn by the woman sitting next to me, and, like her, they were smartly turned out. No cuts on their faces. But each handcuffed at the wrists.

The huge brown-haired man motioned for us to get up and took us to the end of the room. Walking with one shoe was uncomfortable and I wondered if it wouldn't be better to take it off. I felt quite a sharp pain in the ankle of the foot without a shoe.

A nurse led us into a small room with two camp beds. We lay down. A young man came in. He wore a white coat and had a jawline beard. He checked his papers and asked the woman her name. She replied: Jacqueline Beausergent. He asked me for my name, too. He examined my shoeless foot, then my leg, lifting my trousers up to the knee. The nurse helped her out of her coat and cleaned the cuts on her face with cotton wool. Then they switched on a night-light, and left us. The door was wide open and, in the light of the corridor, our man paced up and down. He appeared in the doorway with the regularity of a metronome. She was lying there next to me, her fur coat pulled over her like a blanket. There wouldn't have been room for a bedside table between the two beds. She reached her hand out and squeezed my wrist. I thought of the handcuffs that the two women were wearing earlier and again said to myself that they would end up putting them on us, too.

Out in the corridor, he stopped pacing. He was talking quietly with the nurse. She came into the room, followed by the young man with the jawline beard. They turned on the light and stood at the head of my bed. I turned to the woman and she shrugged under the fur coat, as if to tell me there was nothing we could do, we were trapped, the time to escape had passed. The huge brown-haired man stood motionless in the doorway, his legs slightly apart, his arms folded. He didn't take his eyes off us. He must have been preparing to stop us in case we tried to escape. She smiled at me again, with that same wry smile she had in the police van earlier. I don't know why, but this smile made me uneasy. The fellow with the jawline beard and white coat leaned over me and, with the nurse's help, put a kind of big black muzzle over my mouth and nose. I smelled the ether before losing consciousness.

*

From time to time, I tried to open my eyes, but I kept falling into a half-sleep. Then I had a dim memory of the accident and wanted to turn over and see if she was still there in the other bed. But I didn't have the strength to make the slightest movement—the stillness put me at ease. I remembered the big black muzzle, too. It must have been the ether that put me in this state. I lay still and let myself drift along in the river's current. Her face came to me with total precision, like a large identikit photograph: the even arches of her eyebrows, clear eyes, blonde hair, the cuts on her forehead, cheekbones and the hollow of her cheek. In my half-sleep the huge brown-haired man held up the photo, asking me if I 'knew this person'. I was astonished to hear him speak.

He kept repeating the question with the metallic voice of a talking clock. I studied the face until I thought, yes, I know this person. Or perhaps I had met someone who looked very similar. I could no longer feel the pain in my left foot. That evening I was wearing my old moccasins with crepe rubber soles and stiff leather, which I had cut with scissors because they were too tight and hurt my ankles. I thought about that shoe I had lost, the forgotten shoe left in the middle of the pavement. The shock of the accident brought back the memory of the dog that had been run over long ago, and I could see the sloping avenue in front of the house. The dog used to escape and go to the vacant lot at the end of the avenue. I was afraid that he might get lost, so I kept an eye out for him from my bedroom window. It was often evening when he came walking slowly back up the avenue. Why had this woman become associated with a house where I had spent part of my childhood?

Again, I heard him ask me the same question, 'Do you know this person?' His voice became softer and softer until it was a whisper, as if he was speaking right up against my ear. I stayed still and let myself be carried along by the river, perhaps the same river where we used to walk with the dog. Faces gradually appeared in front of me, and I compared them with the identikit photograph. Of course, that was it: she had a room on the first floor of the house, the last room at the end of the corridor. The same smile, the same blonde hair but worn longer. She had a scar across her left cheekbone, and I suddenly understood why I had thought I recognised her in the police van. The cuts on her face must have reminded me of the scar, only I hadn't realised it then.

Once I had the strength to turn over to the side where she lay on the other bed, I would reach out and touch her shoulder to wake her. She would still be wrapped up in her fur coat. I would ask her all the questions I needed to ask. I would finally find out exactly who she was.

I couldn't see much of the room: only the white ceiling and the window opposite me. Or rather, a bay window, on the right of which a branch swung to and fro. And the blue sky behind the windowpane, a blue so pure that I thought it must be a beautiful winter's day. I had the impression I was in a hotel in the mountains. Once I was able to get up and walk over to the window, I would see that it looked out onto a field of snow, perhaps the start of a ski run. I was no longer carried by the river's current, but was gliding over the snow, a gentle, endless slope, and the air I breathed had the coolness of ether.

The room seemed larger than the one last night in the Hôtel-Dieu, and I hadn't noticed a bay window, or any other window in that kind of storage room where we had been taken after the waiting room. I turned my head. No camp bed, no one else but me. They must have given her a room next to mine, and I would soon see how she was. The huge brown-haired man who I feared would handcuff us to each other was surely not a policeman as I had thought, and we owed him no explanation. He could ask me all the questions he liked, interrogate me for hours; I no longer felt guilty of anything. I was gliding over the snow and the cold air made me slightly euphoric. The accident the night before did not happen by chance. It marked a breach in continuity. The shock was good for me, and it occurred in time for me to make a new start in life.

The door was to my right, beyond the small, white, wooden bedside table where they had left my wallet and passport. And on the metal chair against the wall, I recognised my clothes. At the foot of the chair, my one shoe. I could hear voices on the other side of the door, the voices of a man and a woman conversing calmly. I really had no desire to get up. I wanted to prolong this respite as long as possible. I wondered if I was still in the Hôtel-Dieu, but it didn't feel like it, because of the silence, barely interrupted by the two reassuring voices on the other side of the door. The branch waved to and fro in the window frame. Sooner or later they would come and explain everything to me. I felt absolutely no apprehension, even though I had always been on edge. Perhaps I owed this sudden peacefulness to the ether they made me inhale the night before, or another drug that had eased the pain. In any case, the heaviness I had always felt bearing down on me had lifted. For the first time in my life, I was light and carefree, and that was my real nature. The blue sky at the window evoked one word for me: ENGADIN. I had always needed fresh air, and last night a mysterious doctor, after having examined me, understood that I had to leave for ENGADIN immediately.

I could hear their conversation on the other side of the door, and the presence of these two unseen and unknown people reassured me. Perhaps they were there to watch over me. Again the car appeared suddenly from the shadows, grazed me and collided with the arcade, the door opened and she stumbled out. While we were sitting on the sofa in the hotel lobby and until she squeezed my wrist in the police van, I thought she was drunk. In a police station, they'd say, an ordinary accident like one that was caused by someone 'driving under the influence'. But now I was sure it was something else entirely. It was as if there was someone watching over me without my knowing or as if chance had put something in my path to protect me. And that night, time was running out. I had to be protected from some kind of danger, or be warned about it. A scene came back to me, probably because of the word ENGADIN. A few years earlier, I had seen a fellow hurtling down a steep ski slope and deliberately throw himself against the wall of a chalet and break his leg so he wouldn't have to go to war, the war we called 'Algerian'. In short, he was trying to save his life that day. As for me, apparently I didn't even have a broken leg. Thanks to her, I came out of it relatively unscathed. I needed the shock. It gave me the opportunity to reflect on what my life had been up to that point. I had to admit that I was 'heading for disaster'—to use the words I'd heard others say about me.

Once again my gaze landed on the shoe at the foot of the chair: the big moccasin I had split at the ankle. They must have been surprised when they removed it, before putting me in bed. They were kind enough to put it with the rest of my clothes and lend me the pyjamas I was wearing, blue with white stripes. Where did all this solicitude come from? She must have given them instructions. I couldn't take my eyes off the shoe. Later on, when my life had taken a new course, I would always have to keep it in view, displayed on a mantelpiece or in a glass box, as a souvenir from the past. And to those who wanted to know more about it, I would reply that it was the only thing my parents had left me; yes, as far back as I could remember, I had always walked with one shoe. With this thought, I closed my eyes and sleep came to me in a burst of silent hysterical laughter.

*

A nurse woke me with a tray, which she told me was break-fast. I asked her where exactly I was and she seemed surprised that I didn't know. At the Mirabeau Clinic. When I asked the address of the clinic, she didn't answer. She studied me with an incredulous smile. She thought I was making fun of her. Then she consulted a form she had taken out of the pocket of her white coat and told me that I had to 'leave the premises'. I repeated, which clinic? The floor pitched as it did in my dream. I had dreamed that I was a prisoner on a cargo ship in the middle of the sea. All I wanted was to reach solid ground. The Mirabeau Clinic, Rue Narcisse-Diaz. I didn't venture to ask her which neighbourhood the street was in. Was it near the Hôtel-Dieu? She seemed to be in a hurry and closed the door behind her without giving me any further information. They had bandaged my ankle, knee, wrist and hand. I couldn't bend my left leg, but I managed to dress myself. I put on my one shoe, thinking that it might be difficult to walk in the street but that there was sure to be a bus stop or metro station nearby and I'd soon be back at my place. I decided to lie down again on the bed. I still felt at ease. Would this feeling last long? I was afraid it would disappear as soon as I left the clinic. Looking at the blue sky framed by the window, I convinced myself that they had brought me to the mountains. I had avoided going over to the window, for fear of disappointment. I wanted to remain under the illusion for as long as possible that the Mirabeau Clinic was in a winter sports village in Engadin. The door opened and the nurse appeared. She carried a plastic bag, placed it on the bedside table and left without a word, in one swift movement. In the bag was the shoe I had left behind. They had taken the trouble to go all the way over there and retrieve it from the pavement. Or perhaps she had asked them to get it. I was surprised by such attention on my behalf. Now nothing was stopping me 'leaving the premises', as the nurse had instructed. I felt like walking in the open air.

I was limping a little and held the banister as I went down the long staircase. In the entrance hall, I was about to leave through the glass doors, one side of which stood open, when I noticed the huge brown-haired man. He was sitting on a bench. He waved to me and got up. He was wearing the same coat as the other night. He took me over to the reception desk. They asked for my name. He stood next to me, as if to better monitor my movements, but I was planning on giving him the slip. As quickly as possible. There in the entrance hall rather than out in the street. The woman at reception gave me a sealed envelope with my name written on it.

Then she gave me a discharge form to sign and handed me another envelope, this time with the clinic's letterhead on it. I asked her if I had to pay anything, but she told me that the bill had been taken care of. By whom? In any case, I wouldn't have had enough money. As I was about to cross the hall towards the exit, the huge brown-haired man asked me to sit with him on the bench. He gave me a vague smile and I decided that the fellow probably meant me no harm. He presented me with two sheets of onionskin paper on which some text had been typed. The *report*—I still remember the word he had used—yes, the *report* of the accident. I had to sign my name again, on the bottom of the page. He took a pen out of his coat pocket and even removed the lid for me. He said I could read the text before I signed, but I was in too much of a hurry to get out into the open air. I signed the first sheet. I didn't have to bother with the second; it was a copy for me to keep. I folded it, stuffed it into the pocket of my sheepskin jacket, and got up.

He followed hard on my heels. Perhaps he wanted to put me back in a police van, and there she'd be again, sitting in the same place as the other night? Outside, in the little street that ran down to the quay, there was just one parked car. A man was sitting in the driver's seat. I tried to find the words to take my leave. If I walked off suddenly, he might find my behaviour suspicious and there was a good chance I'd have him on my back again. So I asked him who the woman from the other night was. He shrugged his shoulders and told me that I was bound to see in the *report*, but that it would be better for me and for everyone else if I forgot about the accident. As far as he was concerned the 'case was closed' and he sincerely hoped I thought so, too. He stopped alongside the car and asked, in a cold tone, if I was all right to walk, and if I'd like to be 'dropped off' somewhere. No, I was fine, really. So, without saying goodbye, he got in next to the driver, slammed the door rather savagely and the car moved off towards the quay.

*

The weather was mild, a sunny winter's day. I no longer had any notion of time. It must have been early afternoon. My left leg was hurting a bit. Dead leaves on the pavement. I dreamed that I would come out onto a forest path. I was no longer thinking about the word Engadin, but an even sweeter one, more remote—Sologne. I opened the envelope. Inside was a wad of banknotes. No message or explanation. Why all this money? Perhaps she'd noticed the sorry state of my sheepskin jacket and of my one shoe. Before the split moccasins, I had a pair of big lace-up shoes with crepe rubber soles that I wore even in summer. And it would have been at least the third winter I had worn the old sheepskin jacket. I took the form I had signed out of my pocket. A report or rather a summary of the accident. There was no letterhead from any police branch, nor did it look like a standard administrative form. 'Night-time…a sea-green Fiat automobile…licence plate…coming from the direction of Carrousel Garden and heading into Place des Pyramides…Both taken to the lobby of the Hôtel Régina…Hôtel-Dieu casualty department… Dressings applied to the leg and arm…' There was no mention of the Mirabeau Clinic and I wondered when and how they had transported me there. My surname and my first name were in the summary, as well as my date of birth and my old address. They must have found all this information from my old passport. Her name and surname were also there: Jacqueline Beausergent, and her address: Square de l'Alboni, but they had forgotten to add the street number.

I had never held such a large sum of money in my hands. I would have preferred a note from her, but she was probably not in a state to write after the accident. I assumed that the huge brown-haired guy had taken care of everything. Her husband, perhaps. I tried to remember at what point he had appeared. She was alone in the car. Later on he had walked towards us in the hotel lobby, while we were waiting, sitting next to each other on the sofa. They probably wanted to compensate me for my injuries and felt guilty at the idea of how much worse the accident could have been. I would have liked to reassure them. No, they shouldn't worry on my account. The envelope with the clinic's letterhead contained a prescription signed by a Doctor Besson instructing me to change my dressings regularly. I counted the banknotes again. No more financial worries for a long time. I recalled those last meetings with my father, when I was about seventeen years old, when I never dared to ask him for any money. Life had already drawn us apart and we met up in cafés early in the morning, while it was still dark. The lapels of his suits became increasingly threadbare and each time the cafés were further from the city centre. I tried to remember if I had met up with him in the neighbourhood where I was walking.

I took the report I had signed out of my pocket. So she lived on Square de l'Alboni. I knew the area, as I often got off at the metro station close by. It didn't matter that the number was missing. I'd work it out with her name, Jacqueline Beausergent. Square de l'Alboni was a little further south, next to the Seine. I was in her neighbourhood. That was why they had moved me to the Mirabeau Clinic. She probably knew. Yes, it must have been her idea to have me taken there. Perhaps someone she knew had come to collect us at the Hôtel-Dieu. In an ambulance? I said to myself that at the next phone box I would look her up in the phone directory by street name or I would call directory enquiries. But there was no rush. I had all the time in the world to find her exact address and pay her a visit. It was perfectly justifiable on my part and she surely wouldn't take offence. I had never called at the house of someone I didn't know, but in this case, there were certain details that needed to be clarified, not to mention the wad of banknotes in an envelope, no accompanying message, like a handout thrown to a beggar. You knock someone down in a car at night, and arrange for money to be delivered to him in case he's been crippled. For a start, I didn't want the money. I had never depended on anyone and I was convinced, at that time, that I didn't need anyone. My parents had been of no help at all and the occasional meetings in cafés with my father always ended the same way: we would get up and shake hands. And not once did I have the courage to beg him for money. Especially towards the end, around Porte d'Orléans, when he had lost all the energy and charm that he had on the Champs-Élysées. One morning, I noticed buttons were missing from his navy-blue overcoat.

I was tempted to follow the quay as far as Square de l'Alboni. At each apartment block, I would ask the concierge which floor Jacqueline Beausergent lived on. There couldn't be that many numbers. I recalled her wry smile and how she had squeezed my wrist, as if there were some kind of

complicity between us. It would be best to telephone first.
Not to rush things. I remembered the strange impression
I had in the police van all the way to the Hôtel-Dieu,
that I had already seen her face somewhere else. Before
finding out her phone number, perhaps I would make an
effort to remember. Things were still simple at that time;
I didn't have most of my life behind me. Going back a
few years would be enough. Who knows? I had already
crossed paths with a certain Jacqueline Beausergent, or
the same person going by a different name. I had read
that only a small number of encounters are the product of
chance. The same circumstances, the same faces keep
coming back, like the pieces of coloured glass in a kaleido-
scope, with the play of mirrors giving the illusion that the
combinations are infinitely variable. But in fact the combinations are rather limited. Yes, I must have read that
somewhere, or perhaps Dr Bouvière explained it to us
one evening in a café. But it was difficult for me to
concentrate on these questions for any length of time; I
never felt I had a head for philosophy. All of a sudden,
I didn't want to cross Pont de Grenelle and find myself
south of the river and return, by metro or by bus, to my
room on Rue de la Voie-Verte. I thought I'd walk around

the neighbourhood a bit more. Besides, I had to get used to walking with the dressing on my leg. I felt good there, in Jacqueline Beausergent's neighbourhood. It even felt as if the air was lighter to breathe.

BEFORE THE ACCIDENT, I'd been living for almost a year in Hôtel de la Rue de la Voie-Verte, near Porte d'Orléans. For a long time, I wanted to forget this period of my life, or else remember only the seemingly insignificant details. There was, for example, a man I often passed at around six o'clock in the evening. He was probably returning home from work. All I remember about him is that he carried a black suitcase and walked slowly. One evening, in the large café opposite the Cité Universitaire, I struck up a conversation with a young man sitting next to me who I thought must have been a student. But he worked in a travel agency. He was Madagascan and later I came across his name and a telephone number on a card, among a pile of old papers I was throwing out. His name was Katz-Kreutzer.

I know nothing about him. There were other details...
They were always to do with people I'd come across, barely
glimpsed, and who would remain as mysteries in my mind.
Places too...A little restaurant I would occasionally go to
with my father, near the top of Avenue Foch, on the left. I
searched in vain for it sometime later when I happened to
be passing though the neighbourhood. Or had I dreamed
it? Along with country houses belonging to people whose
names I could no longer recall, near villages I would not be
able to point out on a map, a certain Évelyne I had known
one night on a train. I even started compiling a list, with
approximate dates, of all these lost faces and places, of all
those abandoned projects, like the time I decided to enrol
at the faculty of medicine, but I didn't see it through. My
attempts to catalogue all those plans which never saw the
light of day and which remained forever on hold, a way of
searching for a breach, for vanishing points. Because I'm
reaching the age at which, little by little, life begins to close
in on itself.

I'm trying to recall the colours and the mood of the
period when I lived near Porte d'Orléans. Shades of grey
and black, a mood that seems stifling in retrospect, perpet-
ual autumns and winters. Was it just a coincidence that I

ended up in the area where I had met my father for the last time? Seven o'clock sharp in the morning at La Rotonde café, at the bottom of one of those tall blocks of brick buildings that mark the edge of Paris. Beyond lay Montrouge and a section of the ring road that had just been completed. We didn't have much to say and I knew then that we wouldn't see each other again. We got up and, without shaking hands, left La Rotonde. I was taken aback as I watched him wander off in his navy-blue overcoat towards the ring road. I still wonder which distant suburb he was heading for. Yes, this coincidence is striking now: to have lived for a period in the neighbourhood where our last meetings took place. But at the time, I didn't give it a second thought. I had other things on my mind.

DR BOUVIÈRE IS another one of those fugitive faces from this period. I wonder if he's still alive. Perhaps under another name, in some provincial town, he has found new disciples. Last night, the memory of this man brought on a nervous laugh which I struggled to contain. Had he really existed? Was he not a mirage provoked by lack of sleep, a habit of skipping meals and taking bad drugs? Not at all. There were too many details, too many connections that proved well and truly that a Dr Bouvière, during that time, conducted his meetings from cafés in the fourteenth arrondissement.

Our paths had crossed a few months before the accident. And I must admit that at the Hôtel-Dieu, as they put the black muzzle over my face to administer ether and send me to sleep, I had thought of Bouvière because of his doctor title. I don't know what the title meant, whether it was one of his university ranks or if he was recognised as having completed medical studies. I think Bouvière played on this ambiguity to suggest that his 'learning' covered vast spheres, medicine included.

The first time I saw him, it was not in Montparnasse at one of his meetings, but on the other side of Paris, on the Right Bank, right on the corner of Rue Pigalle and Rue de Douai, in a café called Le Sans Souci. I have to point out what I was doing there, even if I have to come back to it again in more detail one day. Following the example of a French writer known as the 'nocturnal spectator', I frequented certain neighbourhoods in Paris. In the streets at night, I had the impression I was living another life, a more captivating one, or quite simply, that I was dreaming another life.

It was around eight o'clock in the evening, in winter, and there were not many people in the café. My attention was drawn to a couple sitting at one of the tables: he had short silver hair, was around forty, with a bony face and pale eyes. He'd kept his overcoat on. She was a blonde woman of about the same age. Her complexion was translucent, but her features were severe. She spoke to him in a deep, almost masculine voice, and the words I heard sounded like they were being read out, so clear was her articulation. But there was something about her that fitted perfectly with the Pigalle district at that time. Indeed, at first I thought they were the proprietors of one of the nightclubs in the area. Or probably just her, I thought. The man would have stayed behind the scenes. He listened to her as she spoke. He took out a cigarette holder and I was struck by his affectation, a slight movement of the chin, as he put it in his mouth. After a while, the woman stood up and in her smooth voice, articulating each syllable, she said to him, 'Next time, you won't forget my refills, will you,' and this phrase intrigued me. She said it in a dry, almost contemptuous tone and he nodded his head docilely. Then, with an air of confidence, she strode out of the café, without turning back, leaving him looking annoyed.

I watched her leave. She wore a fur-lined raincoat. She walked down Rue Victor-Massé on the left-hand side of the street and I wondered if she would go into the Tabarin. But she didn't. She disappeared. Perhaps into the hotel, further down the street? After all, she was just as likely to be the proprietor of a hotel as of a cabaret or a perfumery. He remained sitting at the table, his head lowered, pensive, the cigarette holder dangling from the corner of his mouth, as if he'd just taken a punch. Under the neon light, his face was veiled in a film of sweat and a kind of grey grease that I've noticed on the faces of men made to suffer by women. Then he got up, too. He was tall, his back slightly stooped. Through the glass, I saw him walk down Rue Pigalle, moving like a sleepwalker.

That was my first encounter with Dr Bouvière. The second was about a fortnight later, in another café, near Denfert-Rochereau. Paris is a big city, but I think you can meet the same person several times and often in places where it would seem most unlikely: in the metro, on the boulevards…Once, twice, three times, you could almost say that fate—or chance—had a hand in it, and was willing a certain meeting or steering your life in a new direction, but you seldom heed its call. You let the face go, and it remains forever unknown, and you feel relief, but also remorse.

I went into the café to buy cigarettes and there was a queue at the counter. The clock on the far wall was show-ing seven o'clock in the evening. At a table beneath it, in the middle of the red moleskin banquette, I recognised Bouvière. There were a few people with him, but they were sitting on chairs. Bouvière was sitting on the banquette by himself, as if the more comfortable spot was his by right. The grey grease and sweat had disappeared from his face, and the cigarette holder was no longer dangling from the corner of his mouth. He was barely the same man. This time he was talking; he even seemed to be delivering a lecture while the others listened in rapture. One of them was scribbling in a large school exercise book. Girls as well as boys. I don't know why I was so curious, perhaps that evening it was the need to answer the question I was asking myself: how could a man transform so dramatically depending on whether he's in Pigalle or Denfert-Rochereau? I had always been very sensitive to the mysteries of Paris.

I sat on the banquette at the table next to theirs, so I could be close to Bouvière. I noticed that they were all drinking coffee, so I ordered one, too. None of them paid me any attention. Bouvière didn't even pause when I knocked the table. I had stumbled over the foot of the table and fallen next to him on the banquette. I listened attentively, but didn't fully understand what he was saying. Certain words didn't have the same meaning when he used them as they do in normal life. I was amazed at how gripped his audience was. They lapped up his words and the fellow with the exercise book didn't pause for a moment from his shorthand scribbling. Bouvière made them laugh from time to time with obscure references that he must have often uttered, like code words. If I have the strength, I will try to remember some of the most characteristic phrases from his lectures. I wasn't receptive to the words he used. They had no resonance, no glimmer of meaning for me. In my memory they are like thin, bleak notes played on an old harpsichord. And besides, without Bouvière's voice to animate them, all that is left are the empty words, whose meaning I can't quite capture. I think Bouvière took them, more or less, from psychoanalysis and far eastern philosophy, but I am reluctant to venture into territory I know little about.

Eventually he turned to me and acknowledged my presence. At first, he didn't see me, and then he asked his audience a question, something like, 'Do you see what I mean?' while staring straight at me. At that moment, I felt like I was melting into the group, and I wondered if, for Bouvière, there was any difference between me and the others. I was certain that in this café, around the same table, his audiences would come and go and, even if there were a handful of loyal followers — an inner circle — different groups would no doubt gather here every evening of the week. He confuses all the faces, all the groups, I said to myself. One more, one less. And every so often he seemed to be talking to himself, like an actor reciting a monologue before a faceless audience. As he felt the attention on him reach its peak, he would draw on his cigarette holder so hard his cheeks became sunken and, without exhaling, he would pause a few seconds to make sure we were all hanging on his every word.

That first night, I arrived towards the end of the meeting. After a quarter of an hour, he stopped speaking, placed a slim, black briefcase on his knees, an elegant model — like the ones in the large leatherwear stores in the Saint-Honoré neighbourhood. He took out a diary bound in red leather. He leafed through it. He said to the person sitting closest to him, a young man with a hawkish face, 'Next Friday at Zeyer at eight o'clock.' And the man jotted it down in a notebook. He appeared to be his secretary and I assumed he was responsible for sending out announcements for meetings. Bouvière stood up, and turned to me again. He smiled warmly, as if to encourage me to keep attending their meetings. As a kind of observer? The others stood up together. I followed suit.

Outside, in Place Denfert-Rochereau, he stood in the middle of the group, exchanging a few words with one and then another, like those slightly bohemian philosophy professors who develop the habit of going for a drink with their more interesting students after class and late into the night. And I was part of the group. They walked with him to his car. A young blonde woman, whose thin, severe face I had noticed earlier, walked beside him. He seemed to be on more intimate terms with her than with the others. She wore a waterproof jacket the same colour as that of the woman in Pigalle, but hers wasn't lined with fur. And it was cold that evening.

At some point he took her arm, which didn't seem to surprise anyone. At the car they exchanged a few more words. I stood a short distance from the rest of the group. The way he put his cigarette holder in his mouth didn't have the same affectation that had struck me in Pigalle. On the contrary, the cigarette holder now had something military about it. He was surrounded by his officers and was issuing his latest orders. The blonde girl was standing so close to him their shoulders were touching. Her face became more and more severe, as if she wanted to keep the others at a distance and demonstrate her pride of place.

He got into the car with the girl, who slammed the door shut. He leaned out of the window and waved goodbye to the group, but at that moment he stared directly at me, so that I imagined the gesture was intended just for me. I was on the edge of the pavement and I leaned towards him. The girl looked at me with a sulky expression. He was getting ready to start the engine. I was gripped by vertigo. The phrase had so intrigued me the other night in Pigalle that I wanted to knock on the window and say to Bouvière, 'You haven't forgotten the refills?' I was saddened by the thought that this phrase would remain a mystery, one among so many other words and faces captured in a moment and which continue to shine in your memory with the glimmer of a distant star, before being erased forever, on the day of your death, without ever revealing their secrets.

I stayed there on the pavement, in the middle of the group. I was embarrassed. I didn't know what to say to them. I ended up smiling at the fellow with the hawkish face. Perhaps he knew more than the others. I asked him, a little abruptly, the name of the girl who had just left in the car with Bouvière. He replied, nonplussed, in a soft, deep voice, that her name was Geneviève. Geneviève Dalame.

I'M TRYING TO remember what I could have been doing so late, on the night of the accident, around Place des Pyramides. I should explain that, during that period, every time I crossed over from the Left Bank I was happy, as if all I needed was to cross the Seine to be lifted out of my stupor. Suddenly there would be electricity in the air. Something was finally going to happen to me.

I probably attach too much importance to topography. I had often wondered why, in the space of a few years, the places where I would meet my father gradually moved from the area around the Champs-Élysées towards Porte d'Orléans. I even remember unfolding a map of Paris in my hotel room on Rue de la Voie-Verte. With a red ballpoint pen, I marked crosses that I used as reference points. It had all started in an area with L'ÉTOILE at the centre of gravity, with exit routes running away to the east in the direction of Bois de Boulogne. Then Avenue des Champs-Élysées. We had slipped imperceptibly past the Madeleine and the Grands Boulevards towards the Opéra neighbourhood. Then further south, near the Palais-Royal for a few months — long enough for me to think that he had finally found somewhere to settle — where I would meet my father at the Ruc Univers. We were getting closer to a border that I tried to mark off on my map. From the Ruc we moved to the Corona café, on the corner of Place Saint-Germain-l'Auxerrois and Quai du Louvre. Yes, I think that's where the border lay.

He always arranged to meet at around nine o'clock at night. The café was about to close. We were the only customers left in the back room. The traffic along the quays had died down by then and we could hear the Saint-Germain-l'Auxerrois clock strike the quarter hours. It was there that I first noticed his threadbare suit and the missing buttons from his navy-blue overcoat. But his shoes were immaculately polished. I wouldn't go as far as to say that he looked like an out-of-work musician, more like an adventurist after a stint in prison. Business was getting worse and worse. The spark and agility of youth had gone. From

Saint-Germain-l'Auxerrois we finished up around Porte d'Orléans. And then, one last time, I watched his silhouette disappear into a foggy November morning—a reddish-brown fog—around Montrouge and Châtillon. He was heading towards these two neighbourhoods, each of which has a fort where they used to shoot people at dawn.

I often found myself, sometime later, making the same journey in reverse. At around nine o'clock at night, I would leave the Right Bank, cross the Seine at Pont des Arts, and find myself at the Corona café. But this time, I was alone at one of the tables in the back room and I no longer needed to find something to say to the shifty-looking guy in the navy-blue overcoat. I began to feel a sense of relief. On the other side of the river I left behind a marshy zone where I was starting to flounder. I had set foot on solid ground. The lights were brighter here. I could hear the neon buzz. Soon I would be walking in the open air, through the arcades, up to Place de la Concorde. The night would be clear and still. The future opened out before me. I was alone at Place de la Concorde and could hear the Saint-Germain-l'Auxerrois clock strike the quarter hours. I couldn't help thinking about Bouvière's disciples and the few meetings I had attended those past weeks. They were always held in cafés around

Denfert-Rochereau. Apart from one evening, further south, Rue d'Alésia, at the Terminus, where I had sometimes met up with my father. That night, I had imagined him and Bouvière meeting. Two very different worlds. Bouvière, a bit pompous, with a whole string of diplomas and protected by his status of doctor and guru. My father, more reckless and whose only education was the street. Both of them crooks, each in his own way.

At the last meeting, Bouvière brought roneos and I learned from the young man with the hawkish face that he gave the same lectures at some university or school of advanced studies whose name I can no longer recall. They all attended the lectures, but I really couldn't bear to sit in a row on those school benches with the others. Boarding school and the barracks were enough for me. On the night that the hawk distributed notes while Bouvière was getting settled on the moleskin banquette, I gestured to him discreetly that I didn't need one. The hawk gave me a disapproving look. I didn't want to upset him, so I took one. Later on I tried to read it in my room but I couldn't follow it beyond the first page. It was as if I could still hear Bouvière's voice. It was neither feminine nor masculine; there was something smooth about it, something cold and smooth, which had no effect on me, but it must have gradually sneaked up on the others, inducing a kind of paralysis that left them under his spell.

Yesterday afternoon his features came back to me with photographic precision: cheekbones, small, pale eyes set deep in their sockets. A skull. Fleshy lips, oddly contoured. And that voice, so cold and smooth…I remember at that time, there were other skulls like his, a few gurus and sages, and sects in which people my age searched for a political doctrine, a strict dogma, or some great helmsman to whom they could devote themselves body and soul. I don't know why I managed to escape these dangers. I was just as vulnerable as the rest. Nothing really distinguished me from all the other disorientated listeners who congregated around Bouvière. I, too, needed some certainties. How on earth had I avoided his trap? Thank goodness for my laziness and indifference. And perhaps I also owe it to my matter-of-fact nature, my connection to concrete details. That man wore a pink tie. And this woman's perfume smelled like tuberose. Avenue Carnot is on an incline. Have you noticed that on certain streets in the late afternoon, the sun is in your eyes? They took me for a fool.

*

They would have been really disappointed if I had admitted to one of the reasons I attended their meetings. Among them I had noticed someone who seemed more intriguing than the others, a certain Hélène Navachine. A brunette with blue eyes. She was the only one who didn't take notes. The blonde girl who was always in Bouvière's shadow regarded her with suspicion, as if she might be a rival, and yet Bouvière never paid her any attention. This Hélène Navachine didn't seem to know any other members of the group and didn't speak to anyone. At the end of the meetings I watched her leave alone, cross the square and disappear into the entrance of the metro. One evening, she had a music theory exercise book on her lap. After the meeting, I asked her if she was a musician, and we walked together, side by side. She earned her living by giving piano lessons, but she hoped to get into the Conservatorium.

That evening I took the metro with her. She told me she lived near Gare de Lyon. So that I could accompany her all the way, I invented a meeting in the neighbourhood. Years later, when I was on the same above-ground metro line, between Denfert-Rochereau and Place d'Italie, I wished for a moment that time would dissolve so that I might find myself sitting, once again, on the seat beside Hélène Navachine. A strong feeling of emptiness then swept over me. For reassurance, I told myself it was because the metro was running above the boulevard and rows of buildings. Once the line went underground again, I would no longer feel that sensation of vertigo and loss anymore. Everything would fall back into place, into the reassuring day-after-day monotony.

That evening, we were almost the only people in the carriage. It was well after rush hour. I asked her why she went to Bouvière's meetings. Without knowing who he was, she had read an article of his on Hindu music that she found enlightening, but the man himself had disappointed her a little and his 'teachings' were not up to the standard of the article. She would give it to me to read if I wanted.

What had led me to the groups around Denfert-Rochereau? Just curiosity. I was intrigued by Dr Bouvière. I wanted to know more about him. What was that Dr Bouvière's life like? She smiled. She had asked herself the same question. First appearances would have it that he had never been married, that he took a liking to particular students of his. But did he really like them? They were always the same type: pale, blonde, severe looking, like young Christian girls bordering on mysticism. It had bothered her at first. She felt as if some girls in the meetings looked down on her, as if she wasn't quite in tune with them. We're bound to get on, I said to her. I'd never felt in tune with anything either. I thought she must have been like me, a bit lost in Paris, no family ties, trying to find some axis by which to direct our lives and sometimes coming across Dr Bouvière types.

There was one episode with Bouvière that had taken us both by surprise. At one of the meetings the week before, his face was bruised and swollen, as if he had been beaten up: he had a black eye and bruises on his nose and around his neck. He made no mention of what had happened and, to allay suspicion, he was even more brilliant than usual. He engaged with his listeners and kept asking if we understood everything he was saying. The secretary with the hawkish face and the blonde girl with transparent skin watched him with concerned expressions throughout the lecture. At the end, the blonde girl held a compress to his face and, with a smile, he let himself be nursed. No one dared ask him anything about it. 'Don't you think it's a bit odd?' asked Hélène Navachine, in the calm, jaded tone of those for whom, since childhood, nothing comes as a shock. I almost told her about the woman I had seen in Pigalle with Bouvière, but I couldn't really imagine her having given him such a beating. Nor any other woman for that matter. No, it must have been something more brutal and disturbing. There was a shady side to Dr Bouvière's life, perhaps a secret he was ashamed of. I shrugged my shoulders and said to Hélène Navachine that it was just another one of the mysteries of Paris.

She lived in one of the big apartment blocks opposite Gare de Lyon. I said I had an hour to wait until my meeting. She said she would gladly have invited me in so I wouldn't have to wait outside, but her mother wouldn't have allowed her to bring someone unannounced to their small apartment at 5 Rue Émile-Gilbert.

*

I saw Hélène Navachine at the next meeting. The bruising had almost disappeared from Dr Bouvière's face and he wore just a small bandaid on his right cheek. We would never find out who had beaten him up. He would never let it slip. Even the young blonde woman who got in the car with him each week would be none the wiser, I was sure of it. Men die with their secrets.

That evening I asked Hélène Navachine why she was

so interested in Hindu music. She said she listened to it because it relieved her of a pressure weighing down on her and it transported her to a place where, finally, she could breathe air that was weightless and clear. And really, it was a silent music. She needed air that was lighter and she needed silence. I understood what she meant. I went with her to her piano lessons. They were mostly in the seventh arrondissement. While I waited for her I went for a walk or, on snowy or rainy afternoons, I took shelter in the café nearest the apartment building she had gone into. The lessons were an hour long. There were three or four of them a day. So, during these breaks, I would walk by myself along the abandoned buildings of the *École militaire*. I was afraid I would lose my memory and get lost without daring to ask the way. There were not many passers-by and what directions exactly would I ask for?

One afternoon, standing at the end of Avenue de Ségur, on the edge of the fifteenth arrondissement, I was seized by panic. I felt like I was melting into the sort of fog that signals snow. I wanted someone to take me by the arm and say soothing words to me: 'No, no, it's nothing, old boy... You must be tired...Let's go and get you a cognac...You'll be all right...' I tried to cling to small concrete details. She had said that she tried to keep things simple for her piano lessons. She made all her students learn the same piece. It was called *Bolero*, by Hummel. She played it for me one night on a piano we found in the basement of a brasserie. It wouldn't be long before I could ask her to whistle Hummel's *Bolero*. A German who must have made a voyage to Spain. I'd be better off waiting for her in front of the building where she was giving a lesson. What a strange neighbourhood… a metaphysical neighbourhood, as Dr Bouvière might have said, in his voice that was so chilling and so smooth. How feeble of me to let myself get into such a state. All it took was a bit of fog with a hint of snow at the Ségur-Suffren crossroad for me to lose heart. Really, I was being pathetic. It could be the memory of snow falling that afternoon when Hélène Navachine came out of the building, but each time I think back to this period of my life, I can smell snow—or rather, a coolness that chills the lungs and ends up getting confused in my mind with the smell of ether.

One afternoon, after her piano lesson, she slipped and fell on a patch of black ice and cut her hand. It was bleeding. We found a pharmacy a little further down the road. I asked for some cotton wool and, instead of 90 per cent alcohol, I asked for a vial of ether. I don't think it was a deliberate mistake. We were sitting on a bench. She took the lid off the vial and, as she soaked the cotton wool to apply to her cut, I was hit by the smell of the ether, so strong and so familiar from my childhood. I put the blue vial in my pocket but the smell still hung around us. It permeated the hotel rooms around Gare de Lyon where we used to end up. We would go there before she went home, or when she'd come and meet me there at around nine o'clock at night.

They didn't ask for your papers at those hotels. There were too many people coming and going because the station was nearby. The clients wouldn't stay long in their rooms; there would always be a train coming soon to take them away. Shadows.

We were handed forms on which to write our names and addresses, but they never checked if they matched a passport or ID card. I filled them in for both of us. I wrote different names and addresses each time. I made a note of them in a diary so I could change the names the next time. I wanted to cover our tracks as well as our real birthdates, since both of us were still minors. Last year, in an old wallet, I found the page on which I had listed our false identities.

Georges Accad 28 Rue de la Rochefoucauld, Paris 9e
Yvette Dintillac 75 Rue Laugier
André Gabison Calle Jorge Juan 17, Madrid
Jean-Maurice Jedlinski Casa Montalvo, Biarritz
and Marie-José Vasse
Jacques Piche Berlin, Steglitz, Orleanstrasse 2
Patrick de Terouane 21 Rue Berlioz, Nice
Suzy Kraay Vijzelstraat 98, Amsterdam

I was told that each hotel passed these forms on to the vice squad, where they would be arranged in alphabetical order. Apparently they have all since been destroyed, but I don't believe it. They remain intact in their filing cabinets. One night, just to kill time, a retired police officer started leafing through these old files and he came across André Gabison's or Marie-José Vasse's form. He wondered why, after more than thirty years, these people remained missing, unknown at their addresses. He would never know the truth of it. A long time ago, a girl used to give piano lessons. In the hotel rooms around Gare de Lyon where we used to meet, I noticed that they still had the blackout curtains from the civil defence, even though it was many years after the war. We could hear the comings and goings in the corridor, doors slamming, phones ringing. Behind the partition walls, conversations went on late into the night; it sounded like travelling businessmen endlessly discussing their jobs. Heavy footsteps in the corridor, people carrying suitcases. And, despite the commotion, we both managed to reach the realm of silence she talked about, in which the air was lighter to breathe. After a while it felt as if we were the only people in the hotel, that everyone else had left. They had all gone to the station opposite to catch a train. The silence was so deep it made me think of the little train station in a country village near a border, lost in the snow.

I REMEMBER AT the Mirabeau Clinic, after the accident, I woke with a start and I didn't know where I was. I tried to find the switch for the bedside lamp. Then, in the stark light, I recognised the white walls, the bay window. I tried to fall asleep again but I was disturbed and restless. All night, people were talking on the other side of the partition. A name kept coming up, in different intonations: JACQUELINE BEAUSERGENT. In the morning I realised I had been dreaming. Only the name JACQUELINE BEAUSERGENT was real, since I had heard it from her own mouth at the Hôtel-Dieu, when the fellow in the white coat had asked us who we were.

The other evening, at the south terminal of Orly airport, I was waiting for some friends who were coming back from Morocco. The plane was delayed. It was past ten o'clock. The large hall leading to the arrival gates was almost deserted. I had the odd feeling that I had arrived at a kind of no man's land in space and time. Suddenly I heard one of those disembodied airport voices repeat three times: 'WOULD JACQUELINE BEAUSERGENT PLEASE PROCEED TO DEPARTURE GATE 624.' I ran the length of the hall. I didn't know what had become of her in the past thirty years, but time no longer mattered. I was under the illusion that there could still be a departure gate for me. The last few passengers were making their way to gate 624, where a man in a dark uniform was standing guard. He asked sharply: 'Do you have your ticket?'

'I'm looking for someone…There was an announcement just a moment ago…Jacqueline Beausergent…'

The last passengers had disappeared. He shrugged his shoulders. 'She must have boarded long ago, sir.'

'Are you sure? Jacqueline Beausergent…' I repeated.

He was blocking the way. 'You can see very well there's no one left, sir.'

EVERYTHING ABOUT THE period before the accident is confused in my memory. Days merged into one another in a haze. I was waiting for the voltage to increase to see more clearly. When I think back to it now, only Hélène Navachine's silhouette emerges from the fog. I remember she had a beauty spot on her left shoulder. She told me she was going to London for a few days because she'd been offered a job there and she was going to find out if it was really what she wanted.

I went with her the evening she caught the train at Gare du Nord. She sent me a postcard telling me that she would soon be coming back to Paris. But she never came back. Three years ago, I received a telephone call. A woman's voice said, 'Hello, I'm calling from the Hôtel Palym…There is someone here who would like to speak to you, sir...' The Hôtel Palym was almost opposite her place, in the little street from which you could see the Gare de Lyon clock. We'd taken a room there once under the names Yvette Dintillac and Patrick de Tourane. 'Are you still on the line, sir?' The woman said. 'I'm putting you through...' I was sure it would be her. Once again, we would be meeting between piano lessons and the students would play Hummel's *Bolero* until the end of time. As Dr Bouvière liked to say, life is an eternal return. There was static on the line and it sounded like the murmur of wind through leaves. I waited, gripping the handset to avoid making the slightest movement that might break the thread stretching back through the years. 'Putting you through, sir...' I thought I heard the sound of furniture being knocked over or someone falling down the stairs.

'Hello...Hello...Can you hear me?' A man's voice. I was disappointed. Still the interference on the line. 'I was a friend of your father's...Can you hear me?' I kept saying yes, but he was the one who couldn't hear me. 'Guy Roussotte... My name is Guy Roussotte...Perhaps your father mentioned me...Your father and I worked together at the Bureau Otto... Can you hear me?' He seemed to be asking the question for form's sake without really caring if I could hear him or not.

'Guy Roussotte…Your father and I had an office together…'
It was as if he was calling from one of those bars on the
Champs-Élysées fifty years ago when the clamour of conversation revolved around black-market dealings, women and
horses. His voice was becoming increasingly muffled and
only fragments of sentences reached me: 'Your father…
Bureau Otto…meet…a few days at the Hôtel Palym…
where I could reach him…Just tell him: Guy Roussotte…
the Bureau Otto…from Guy Roussotte…a phone call…
Can you hear me?…'

How did he get my phone number? I wasn't in the
phone book. I imagined this ghost calling from a room at the
Hôtel Palym, perhaps the same room that Yvette Dintillac
and Patrick de Tourane stayed in one night long ago. What
a strange coincidence…The voice was now too faint, and
the sentences too disjointed. I wondered if it was my father
he wanted to see, believing him still of this world, or if it was
me. Soon after, I could no longer hear his voice. Again, the
sound of a piece of furniture being knocked over or someone
falling down the stairs. Then the dial tone, as if the phone
had been hung up. It was already eight o'clock at night and
I didn't have the energy to call the Hôtel Palym back. I was
really disappointed. I had hoped to hear Hélène Navachine's

voice. What could have become of her, after all this time? The last time I saw her in a dream, it was interrupted before she had time to give me her address and phone number.

*

The same winter that I heard the faraway voice of Guy Roussotte, I had an unfortunate experience. Strive as you might for over thirty years to make your life clearer and more harmonious than it was earlier on, there's always the risk that an incident will suddenly drag you backwards. It was in December. For about a week, whenever I went out or returned home, I noticed a woman standing motionless a few metres from the door of my apartment building or on the pavement opposite. She was never there before six o'clock in the evening. A tall woman, dressed in a sheep-skin coat, wearing a wide-brimmed hat and carrying a brown shoulder bag. She kept watching me as she stood there in silence. She looked menacing. From which forgotten child-hood nightmare could this woman have emerged? And why now? I leaned out the window. She was waiting on the pave-ment, as though she was standing guard over the front of the building. But I hadn't switched on the light in my room so she couldn't possibly have seen me. With the big shoulder bag, hat and boots, she looked as though she had once been the canteen cook for an army that had disappeared long ago, but had left many corpses behind. I was afraid that from then on, and until the end of my life, she would be standing guard wherever I lived and that it would be pointless moving house. She would find my new address every time.

One night, I came home later than usual and she was still there, motionless. I was about to push open the door of the building when she walked slowly towards me. An old woman. She stared at me harshly as if to make me ashamed of something or remind me of an error I might have made. I held her gaze in silence. I ended up wondering what I might be guilty of. I crossed my arms and said in a calm voice, articulating each syllable, that I would like to know what she wanted from me.

She raised her chin and from her mouth came a torrent of insults. She called me by my first name and addressed me with the familiar *tu*. Were we somehow related? Perhaps I had known her long ago. The wide-brimmed hat accentuated the hardness of her face and, in the yellow light of the streetlamp, she looked like a very old German poseur by the name of Leni Riefenstahl. Life and emotions had left no trace on this mummy's face, yes, the mummy of a nasty capricious little girl from eighty years ago. She kept staring at me with her raptor eyes and I didn't look away. I gave her a big smile. It felt like she was about to bite and infect me with her venom, but beneath this aggression there was something false, like the lifeless performance of a bad actress. Again, she heaped insults on me. She was leaning against the door of the building to block my way. I kept smiling at her and realised that it was making her increasingly exasperated. But I wasn't scared of her. Gone were the childhood terrors, in the dark, of a witch or death opening the bedroom door. 'Could you lower your voice a little, madame?' I said, in a courteous tone that surprised even me. She, too, seemed taken aback by the calmness of my voice. 'Excuse me, but I'm no longer used to voices as loud as yours.' I saw her features contract and her eyes dilate in a split second. She stuck out her chin defiantly—a very heavy, prominent chin.

I smiled at her. Then she threw herself on me. With one hand she gripped my shoulder and with the other she tried to scratch my face. I tried to free myself, but she was really heavy. I felt my childhood terrors gradually return. For over thirty years, I had made sure that my life was as well ordered as a formal French garden. With its wide walkways, lawns and hedges, the garden had covered over a swamp where I had almost gone under long ago. Thirty years of striving. All of it just for this Medusa figure to stand in wait for me one night on the street and pounce on me...This old woman was going to suffocate me. She was as heavy as my childhood memories. I was being smothered in a shroud and it was useless to fight. No one could help me. A little further down, on the square, there was a police station, with some officers on guard duty out the front. It would all end up in a paddy wagon and a police station. It had been inevitable for a long time. Besides, at the age of seventeen, when my father had me arrested because he wanted to get rid of me, it happened around here, near the church. More than thirty years of futile striving just to come right back to where it started, in neighbourhood police stations. How sad...They looked like two drunks fighting in the street, one of the policemen would say. They would sit us on a bench, the old woman and me, like everyone who'd been caught in night round-ups, and I would have to state my name and address. They would ask me if I knew her. 'She's trying to pass herself off as your mother,' the superintendent would say, 'but according to her papers, you're not related. And besides, your mother's identity is unknown. You're free to go, sir.' It was the same superintendent my father had handed me over to when I was seventeen. Dr Bouvière was right: life is an eternal return.

A cold rage came over me and I kneed the old woman sharply in the belly. Her grip loosened. I pushed her hard. Finally, I could breathe…I had taken her by surprise, she didn't dare come near me again; she remained motionless, on the edge of the pavement, staring at me with her small, intense eyes. Now it was her turn to be on the defensive. She tried to smile at me, a horrible artificial smile that was at odds with the harshness of her expression. I crossed my arms. Then, seeing that the smile didn't work on me, she pretended to wipe away a tear. At my age, how could I have been terrified of this ghost and believe for an instant that she still had the power to drag me down? That period of police stations was well and truly over.

She was no longer standing guard over the apartment building during the days that followed and, so far, she's given no further sign of life. But later that night, I saw her again from the window. She didn't seem the least bit affected by our fight. She paced up and down the median strip. She went back and forth over quite a short distance, but with a lively, almost military gait. Very erect, her chin high. Every now and again she would look over at the façade of the apartment building to check if she still had an audience. And then she would begin to limp. At first she was practising as if for a rehearsal. Gradually, she found her rhythm. I watched her move off limping and then disappear, but she overplayed the part of the old canteen cook searching for a routed army.

THREE YEARS AGO, roughly around the same time the old woman attacked me, but in June or July, I was walking along Quai de la Tournelle. A sunny Saturday afternoon. I was looking at books in the bouquinistes' stalls. Suddenly my eyes fell upon three volumes prominently displayed and held together by a large red elastic band. The yellow cover, the author's name and the title in black characters on the first volume gave me a pang of emotion: *Screen Memories* by Fred Bouvière. I removed the elastic band. Two more books by Bouvière: *Drugs and Therapeutics* and *The Lie and the Confession*. He had referred to them on several occasions during the meetings at Denfert-Rochereau. Three unobtainable books, which he said with a certain irony were his 'early works'. Their publication dates were printed at the bottom of the covers with the name of the publisher: Au Sablier. Bouvière would have been very young then, barely twenty-two or twenty-three.

I bought the three volumes and discovered a dedication on the flyleaf of *The Lie and the Confession*: 'For Geneviève Dalame. This book was written when I was her age, during curfew hours. Fred Bouvière.' The other two didn't have dedications but, like the first, they bore the name 'Geneviève Dalame' in blue ink on the title page, with an address: 4 Boulevard Jourdan. It all came back to me: the face of the blonde girl with very pale skin, who was always in Bouvière's shadow and sat next to him on the front seat of his car at the end of the meetings; the guy with the hawkish face saying to me in a low voice: 'Her name is Geneviève Dalame.' I asked the bouquiniste where he had found the books. He shrugged—Oh, someone moving house... Remembering the way Geneviève Dalame contemplated Bouvière, with her blue-eyed gaze, and hung on his every word, I thought it was impossible that she would have got rid of these three books. Unless she wanted to make a sudden break with an entire period of her life. Or she had died. Four Boulevard Jourdan. It was just around the corner from me when I was staying in Hôtel de la Rue de la Voie-Verte. But

I didn't need to check; I knew the apartment block hadn't been there for about fifteen years and that Rue de la Voie-Verte had changed name.

I remembered that, one day back then, I was waiting to catch the number 21 bus at Porte Gentilly and she came out of the little apartment block, but I didn't dare approach her. She was waiting for the bus, too, and we were the only ones at the bus stop. She didn't recognise me, which was entirely understandable: in the meetings she only had eyes for Bouvière and all the other members of the group were nothing but blurred faces in the glowing halo he projected around himself.

When the bus started moving, we were the only passengers, and I sat on the seat opposite her. I had a clear memory of the name that the hawk had whispered in my ear a few days before. Geneviève Dalame. She was absorbed in a book covered with glassine paper, perhaps the one that Bouvière had dedicated to her and written during curfew hours. I didn't take my eyes off her. I had read, I can't recall where, that if you stare at someone, even from behind, they will notice your presence. With her it took a long time. She didn't even vaguely notice me until the bus was going along Rue Glacière.

'I've seen you in Dr Bouvière's meetings,' I said. By

uttering his name I thought I would gain her favour, but she gave me a guarded look. I tried to think of something to say to win her over. 'It's crazy…' I said, 'Dr Bouvière answers all of life's questions.' And I took on a preoccupied air, as if to merely pronounce the name Bouvière was enough to detach oneself from the everyday world and from the bus we were on. She seemed reassured. We had the same guru, we shared the same rituals and the same secrets.

'Have you been going to the meetings for long?' she asked.

'A few weeks.'

'Would you like to have more personal contact with him?' She asked the question with a certain condescension, as if she was the sole possible intermediary between Bouvière and the mass of disciples.

'Not just yet,' I said, 'I'd prefer to wait a little longer…' My tone of voice was so solemn that she could no longer doubt my sincerity.

She smiled at me and I believe I even detected, in her big pale-blue eyes, a kind of tenderness. But I was under no illusion. I owed it all to Bouvière.

She wore a man's watch, which contrasted with the slenderness of her wrist. The black leather strap wasn't tight enough. Too roughly, she stuffed her book into her bag. The watch slipped and fell off. I leaned down to pick it up. It must have been an old watch of Bouvière's, I thought. She had asked if she could wear it so that she would always have something of his with her. I wanted to help her tighten the strap around her wrist, but it was clearly too big for her. At the base of her wrist, close to the veins, I noticed a recent scar, still pink, a row of little blisters. At first I felt uneasy. The scar didn't fit with this sunny winter's day, sitting on a bus with a blonde, blue-eyed girl. I was just a simple fellow with a taste for happiness and formal French gardens. Dark ideas often crossed my mind, but they were involuntary. It was perhaps the same for her, too. Her smile and her gaze suggested that before meeting Dr Bouvière, she had a care-free nature. He was probably responsible for her losing her love of life.

She realised that I'd seen her scar and she held her hand pressed flat against her knee to hide it. I wanted to talk to her about innocuous things. Was she still studying or had she already found a job? She explained that she had been working as a typist in an office called Opéra Intérim. All of a sudden she spoke naturally and without any of the affecta-tion she had when we talked about the doctor. I ended up convincing myself that, before coming across him, she had been a perfectly simple girl. And I regretted not having met her then.

I asked her how long she had been going to the meetings. Almost a year. At first, it was difficult, she didn't understand a lot of it. She knew nothing about philosophy. She had left school before the baccalauréat, at fifteen. She felt that she wasn't good enough and this feeling threw her into a 'crisis of despair'. Perhaps those words were a way of making me understand why she had the scar on her wrist. Dr Bouvière had helped her overcome this lack of confidence. It had been painful, but, thanks to him, she had managed to get through it. She was truly grateful to him for helping her get to a level that, alone, she would never have been able to reach.

Where had she met him? Oh, in a café. She was eating a sandwich before going back to work at the office. He was preparing one of his classes that he gave at the Hautes Études. When he found out she was a typist, he asked her to type up a text for him. I was about to tell her that I had met Bouvière for the first time in a café as well. But I was afraid of bringing up a painful topic. Perhaps she knew of the existence of the woman with the fur-lined raincoat, the one who said: 'Next time, you won't forget my refills, will you.' What if this woman was the cause of the scar on her wrist? Or was it just Bouvière, whose love life at first seemed rather strange to me…

I wanted to know what stop she was getting off at. Petits-Champs — Danielle Casanova. My ticket was for Gare du Luxembourg, but that didn't matter. I had decided to stay with her until she got off. She was heading for Opéra Intérim, but soon, she said, she would be leaving that job. The doctor had promised her 'full-time work': typing up his class notes and articles, arranging his meetings, and preparing notifications and memos to send out to the different groups. She was happy to have a real job that finally gave her life some meaning.

'So you're going to devote yourself entirely to the doctor?' The question slipped out, and I immediately regretted it. She stared at me, a certain steeliness in her pale-blue eyes. I wanted to make up for my tactlessness with a more general remark: 'You know, gurus don't always realise how much power they hold over their followers.' She softened her gaze. I got the impression she was no longer focused on me and was lost in her thoughts.

'You think so?' she asked. I was moved by how much confusion and candour there was in her question. A real job that would finally give her life some meaning…In any case, she had wanted to end it, her life, judging by the scar on her wrist. I would have loved her to confide in me. I dreamed, for a moment, that on the bus she brought her face close to mine and spoke at length up close to my ear so that no one else could hear.

Once more, she looked at me suspiciously. 'I don't agree with you,' she said abruptly. 'Personally, I need a guru…' I nodded. I had no response to give her. We had arrived at the Palais-Royal. The bus passed in front of the Ruc-Univers where I had often sat with my father, out on the terrace. He never said anything either, and we parted without breaking the silence. A lot of congestion. The bus lurched along. I should have taken the opportunity to ask her questions quickly and to learn more about this girl, Geneviève Dalame, but she seemed preoccupied. All the way to Petits-Champs—Danielle-Casanova, we didn't exchange a single word. And then we got off the bus. On the pavement, she shook my hand distractedly, with her left hand, the one with the watch and the scar. 'See you at the next meeting,' I said. But at the meetings after that, she always ignored my presence. She walked up Avenue Opéra and I quickly lost sight of her. There were far too many people about at that hour.

LAST NIGHT, I dreamed for the first time about one of the saddest experiences of my life. When I was seventeen years old, in order to get rid of me, my father called the police one afternoon, and a police van was waiting for us in front of the apartment block. He handed me over to the superintendent, saying that I was a 'thug'. I would rather forget this experience but, in my dream last night, a detail that had been erased with all the rest came back and rattled me, forty years on, like a time bomb. I'm sitting on a bench at the back of the police station, waiting, with no idea what they're going to do with me. Every now and again I would fall into a half-sleep. From midnight onwards, I frequently hear the sound of a car engine and doors slamming. Police officers push a motley group into the room, some of them well dressed, others who look more like homeless people. A round-up. They give their names. Gradually they disappear into a room; I can only see the wide-open door. The last one to present herself to the fellow tapping at the typewriter is a young woman, with chestnut hair, dressed in a fur coat. Several times the police officer makes a mistake spelling her name, and she repeats wearily: JACQUELINE BEAUSERGENT.

Before she goes into the room next door, our eyes meet.

I WONDER IF, on the night when the car knocked me over, I hadn't just accompanied Hélène Navachine to her train at Gare du Nord. Whole sections of our lives end up slipping into oblivion and, sometimes, tiny little sequences in between as well. And on this strip of old film, spots of mould cause shifts in time and give the impression that two events occurring months apart took place on the same day or even simultaneously. How can any sense of chronology be established as we watch these truncated images scroll past before us, overlapping chaotically in our memories, or following one after the other, sometimes slowly, sometimes jolting, in the middle of blanks. It leaves my mind reeling.

It appears I must have been walking back from Gare du Nord that night. If not, why would I have found myself

sitting on a bench so late at night, near Square de la Tour
Saint Jacques, in front of the night bus station? A couple was
also waiting at the station. The man started speaking to me
in an aggressive tone. He wanted me to go with them, him
and the woman, to a hotel. The woman said nothing and
seemed embarrassed. He took me by the arm and tried to
pull me along. He pushed me towards her. 'She's nice, isn't
she? And you haven't seen everything yet.' I tried to get away
from him, but he wouldn't let me go. Each time, he'd grab
me by the arm. The woman smiled contemptuously. He
must have been drunk; he thrust his face into mine when he
spoke to me. He didn't smell of alcohol, but of a strange eau
de toilette, Aqua di selva. I shoved him away violently with
my elbow. He turned to me, open-mouthed, crestfallen.

I started down Rue de la Coutellerie, a small, deserted
street that runs at an angle just before the Hôtel de Ville.
Over the years since then—and even as recently as today—I
have returned to this street to try to understand the uneasiness that it caused me the first time. The feeling of unease
is still there. Or rather, the feeling of slipping into a parallel
world, outside time. All I have to do is walk along this road to
realise that the past is gone for good, without really knowing
which present I exist in. It's a simple through road that cars

roar down at night. A forgotten street that no one has ever thought much about. That night, I noticed a red light on the left-hand side. The place was called Les Calanques. I went in. Light came from a paper lantern hanging from the ceiling. Four people were playing cards at one of the tables. A brown-haired man with whiskers stood up and came over to me. 'For dinner, sir? On the first floor.' I followed him up the stairs. Here, too, only one table was occupied, also by four people, two women and two men—close to the bay window. He showed me to the first table on the left, at the top of the stairs. The others took no notice of me at all. They were talking quietly, murmurs and occasional laughter. Gifts lay open on the table, as if they were celebrating one of their birthdays or Christmas or New Year's Eve. On the red tablecloth was the menu. I read: Fish Waterzooi. The names of the other dishes were written in tiny letters that I couldn't make out under the bright, almost white light. Next to me, there were stifled bursts of laughter.

FISH WATERZOOI. I wondered who the regulars of this place could be. Members of a brotherhood who passed on the address to one another in hushed voices or, as time had no meaning in this street, had these people lost their way and were now gathered around a table for eternity? I no longer knew how I ended up here. I was probably uneasy about Hélène Navachine leaving. And it was a Sunday night, and Sunday nights leave strange memories, like brief interludes of nothingness in our lives. You had to go back to school or to the barracks. You waited on the platform of a station whose name you can't remember. A little later, you slept badly under the blue night-lights in a dormitory.

And now, there I was at Les Calanques sitting at a table covered with a red tablecloth, and fish waterzooi was on the menu. Over by the window, there were stifled bursts of laughter. One of the two men had put on a black astrakhan hat. His glasses and thin French face contrasted with the Russian or Polish lancer's hat. A shapka. Yes, it was called a shapka. He leaned over to the blonde woman sitting next to him to kiss her on the shoulder, but she didn't let him. The others laughed. With the best will in the world I would not have been able to join in their laughter. If I'd gone over to their table, I don't believe they would have seen me and, if I'd spoken to them, they wouldn't even have heard the sound of my voice. I tried to hold on to concrete details. Les Calanques, 4 Rue de la Coutellerie. Perhaps my uneasiness came from the topographical position of the street. It led down to the large buildings of the police headquarters on the banks of the Seine. There was no light in any of the windows of those buildings. I stayed sitting at the table, to delay the moment when I'd end up alone again in that area. Even the thought of the lights of Place du Châtelet gave me no comfort. Nor the thought of Saint-Germain-l'Auxerrois further along the deserted quays. The other man had taken off his shapka and was mopping his brow. No one came to take my order. But I would have been incapable of swallowing a thing. Fish Waterzooi in a restaurant called Les Calanques...There was something unsettling about this combination. I was less and less sure that I could overcome the distress of Sunday nights.

*

Outside, I wondered if I ought to go and wait for the night bus again. But I was overcome with panic at the prospect of going back to my hotel room alone. The Porte d'Orléans neighbourhood suddenly seemed bleak, perhaps because it reminded me of a recent past: the silhouette of my father walking away towards Montrouge as if to meet a firing squad, and of all our missed meetings at the Zeyer, the Rotonde and the Terminus in this hinterland...That was the time of evening I would have most needed Hélène Navachine's company. I would have found it reassuring to go back to my room with her and we could even have made the journey on foot through the dead Sunday-night streets. We would have laughed harder than the fellow in the shapka and his friends earlier at Les Calanques.

I tried to muster some courage by telling myself that not everything was that gloomy in the Porte d'Orléans neighbourhood. On summer days there, the great bronze lion would sit under the foliage and each time I looked at him from a distance, his presence on the horizon reassured me. He kept watch over the past, but also over the future. That night, the lion would be a landmark for me. I trusted this sentinel.

I quickened my pace as far as Saint-Germain-l'Auxerrois. When I reached the arcades of Rue de Rivoli, it was as if I had suddenly been woken up. Les Calanques... The guy in the shapka who tried to kiss the blonde woman... Walking the length of the arcades, I felt as though I had reached open air again. To the left was the Palais du Louvre and, just up ahead, the Tuileries Gardens of my childhood. As I made my way towards Place de la Concorde, I would try to picture what was on the other side of the railings in

the darkness: the first ornamental lake, the open-air thea-
tre, the merry-go-round, the second ornamental lake...Just a
few more steps and I would breathe in the sea air. Straight
ahead. And the lion at the end, seated, keeping watch, in
the middle of the crossroad...That night, the city was more
mysterious than usual. I had never experienced such a
profound silence around me. Not a single car. A moment
later, I would cross Place de la Concorde without a thought
about green or red lights, just as one would cross a prairie. I
was in a dream again, but a more peaceful one than earlier
at Les Calanques. The car appeared just as I reached Place
des Pyramides and the pain in my leg told me I was about
to wake up.

IN THE ROOM at the Mirabeau Clinic, after the accident, I had time to think things over. First of all, I remembered the dog that had been run over one afternoon when I was a child; then an episode from the same period came back to me little by little. I think I'd avoided dwelling on it until then. Only the smell of ether would bring it back to me occasionally, that monochromatic smell that carries you to a fragile tipping point between life and death. Coolness and the impression of finally breathing in the open air, but also, sometimes, the weight of a shroud. The previous night, at the Hôtel-Dieu, when the fellow put a muzzle over my face to send me to sleep, I remembered that I had gone through it all before. The same night, the same accident, the same smell of ether.

It was outside a school. The playground looked out onto an avenue on a slight incline, lined with trees and houses, but I no longer knew if they were mansions, country houses or detached suburban houses. Throughout my childhood, I had stayed in so many different places that I ended up getting them confused in my mind. My memory of this avenue had perhaps become mixed up with that of an avenue in Biarritz or of a sloping road in Jouy-en-Josas. During the same period, I had lived in both places, and I think the dog was run over on Rue Docteur-Kurzenne, in Jouy-en-Josas.

I was leaving class at the end of the afternoon. It must have been winter. It was dark. I was waiting on the pavement for someone to come and collect me. Soon there was no one else left. The school gate was closed. There was no light at the windows. I didn't know the way home. I tried to cross the avenue, but as soon as I stepped off the pavement a van braked suddenly and knocked me down. My ankle was injured. They laid me down in the back of the van under the tarpaulin. One of the two men from the van was with me. As the engine started up, a woman got in. I knew her. We lived in the same house. I can still see her face. She was young, about twenty-five, blonde or light brown hair, a scar on her cheek. She leaned over me and held my hand. She was out of breath, as if she had been running. She was explaining to the man next to us that she was late because her car had broken down. She said to him that she *came from Paris*. The van stopped alongside the railings of a garden. One of the men carried me and we crossed the garden. She kept hold of my hand. We went into the house. I was laid down on a bed. A room with white walls. Two nuns leaned over me, their faces taut in their white wimples. They put the same black muzzle over my nose as the one at the Hôtel-Dieu. And before falling asleep, I smelled the monochromatic odour of ether.

*

That afternoon, once I'd left the clinic, I followed the quay towards Pont de Grenelle. I was trying to remember what had happened back then, when I woke up at the convent. After all, the white-walled room where I had been taken looked like the one at the Mirabeau Clinic. And the smell of ether was the same as at the Hôtel-Dieu. That could help me get to the bottom of it. They say that smells bring back the past best, and the smell of ether always had a curious effect on me. It seemed to be the very essence of my child-hood, but as it was bound up with sleep and the numbing of pain, the images that it unveiled clouded over again almost simultaneously. It was surely because of this that my child-hood memories were so confused. Ether made me both remember and forget.

Outside school, the van with the tarpaulin, the convent...I searched for other details. I could see myself next to the woman in a car: she opened a door, the car went down a driveway...She had a room on the first floor of the house, the last one at the end of the corridor. But these frag-ments of memory were so vague that I couldn't hold on to them. Only her face was clear, with the scar on her cheek, and I was truly convinced that it was the same face as the one from the other night, at the Hôtel-Dieu.

Going along the quay, I came to the corner of Rue de l'Alboni, at the spot where the overground metro inter-sects the road. The square was a little further on, at right angles to the road. I stopped, on a whim, in front of a huge building with a black wrought-iron glass door. I was tempted to go through the porte-cochère, to ask the concierge for Jacqueline Beausergent's floor, and if she did indeed live there, to ring at her door. But it really wasn't like me to show up unannounced at people's houses. I had never asked for help or requested anything from anyone.

How much time had passed between the accident outside the school and the one the other night at Place des Pyramides? Fifteen years, if that. Both the woman from the police van and the one at the Hôtel-Dieu seemed young. We don't change much in fifteen years. I climbed the steps up to Passy metro station. Waiting for the train on the platform of the little station, I searched for clues that could tell me if this woman from Square de l'Alboni was the same as the one fifteen years ago. And I would have to put a name to the place with the school, the convent and the house where I must have lived for a while, where she had her room at the end of the corridor. It was during the time when we went to stay in Biarritz and Jouy-en-Josas. Before? In between the two? In chronological order, first it was Biarritz then Jouy-en-Josas. And after Jouy-en-Josas, back to Paris and memories that became clearer and clearer, because I had reached what they call the age of reason, around seven years old. Only my father would have been able to give me some vague details, but he had vanished without a trace. So it was up to me to work it out, and that seemed perfectly natural to me anyway. The metro crossed the Seine towards the Left

Bank. It passed alongside façades whose every lit window seemed an enigma to me.

To my surprise, one weekday evening before the accident, I bumped into Dr Bouvière on the metro. He wasn't surprised in the slightest by our meeting and he explained that the same situations, the same faces, often reappear in our lives. He told me he would develop the theme of the 'eternal return' in one of our next meetings. I felt that he was on the brink of confiding in me. 'You must have been surprised to see me in such a state the other day.' He stared at me almost tenderly. There was not a trace of bruising left on his face or neck. 'You see, my boy...There is something that I have been hiding from myself for a long time... something I have never admitted openly.' Then he collected himself. He shook his head. 'Excuse me...' He smiled at me. He was clearly relieved to have stopped himself at the last moment from making some grave confession. He proceeded to talk too volubly about insignificant things, as if he wanted to throw me off track. He stood up and got off at Pigalle station. I was a little worried about him.

*

When I got out of the metro that afternoon, I dropped into a pharmacy. I handed over the prescription I'd been given at the clinic and asked how I should apply the dressing. The pharmacist wanted to know how I'd sustained my injury. When I explained that I'd been hit by a car, he said, 'I hope you're going to press charges.' He insisted: 'So, have you pressed charges…?' I didn't dare show him the piece of paper I had signed at the Mirabeau Clinic. The piece of paper seemed odd. I planned to read it again in my room with a clear head. As I left the pharmacy, he said, 'And don't forget to disinfect the wound with Mercurochrome every time you change the dressing.'

When I got back to the hotel, I telephoned directory enquiries to find out Jacqueline Beausergent's phone number. Unknown at every number on Square de l'Alboni. My room seemed smaller than normal, as if I had returned after years away or even as if I had lived there in a previous life. Could it be that the accident the other night had caused such a fracture in my life that there was now a before and an after? I counted the banknotes. In any case, I had never been so rich. I could take a break from the exhausting buying and selling all over Paris, flogging to one bookshop what I had just bought at another for a tiny profit.

My ankle hurt. I didn't have the energy to change the dressing. I lay down on my bed, hands crossed under my head, and tried to think about the past. I wasn't used to it. For a long time, I had tried to forget my childhood, never having felt much nostalgia for it. I didn't possess a single photo or any physical evidence from that period, apart from an old vaccination card. Yes, thinking about it, the episode outside the school with the van and the nuns came in between Biarritz and Jouy-en-Josas. So I would have been six years old. After Jouy-en-Josas, it was Paris and the primary school on Rue du Pont-de-Lodi, then different boarding schools and barracks across France: Saint Lô, Haute-Savoie, Bordeaux, Metz, Paris again, where I am now. In fact, the only mystery in my life, the only link that didn't connect with the others, was the first accident with the van and the young woman or young girl who was late that evening *because she had broken down coming from Paris.* And it took the shock of the other night at Place des Pyramides for this forgotten episode to rise to the surface once again. What would Dr Bouvière have thought of it? Could he have used it as an example, along with so many others, to illustrate the theme of the eternal return in the next meeting at Denfert-Rochereau? But it wasn't only this. It also seemed that a breach had opened up in my life onto an unknown horizon.

I got up and from the very top shelf of the cupboard I took down the navy-blue cardboard box in which I kept all the old pieces of paper that would later bear witness to my time on earth. A copy of my birth certificate, which I had just obtained from Boulogne-Billancourt Town Hall in order to obtain a passport; an academic certificate from Grenoble proving that I had passed the baccalauréat; a membership card for the Animal Protection Society; and in my military record book: my baptism certificate from Saint Martin's Parish in Biarritz and the very old vaccination card. I opened it up and read for the first time the list of vaccinations and their dates: a certain Dr Valat had given one of them in Biarritz. Then, six months later, another vaccine, indicated by the stamp of a Dr Divoire, in Fossombronne-la-Forêt, Loir-et-Cher. Then another, many years later, in Paris… I had found a clue. It could have been a needle lost forever in a haystack, or, if I was lucky, a thread that I could trace back through time: Dr Divoire, Fossombronne-la-Forêt.

Then I re-read the report of the accident that the huge brown-haired man had given me outside the clinic, of which he had kept a copy. At the time I hadn't realised that it was written in my own name and began: 'I, the undersigned…'

And the terms used implied that I was responsible for the accident... 'As I was crossing Place des Pyramides, alongside the arcades on Rue de Rivoli and going towards Place de la Concorde, I paid no attention to the approaching sea-green Fiat automobile, licence plate 3212FX75. The driver, Jacqueline Beausergent, tried to avoid me, resulting in a collision with one of the arcades of the square...' Yes, that must be the truth of it. The car wasn't going fast, and I should have looked left before crossing, but that night, I was in an altered state of mind. Jacqueline Beausergent. Directory enquiries had told me that there was no one by this name in Square de l'Alboni. But that was because she wasn't in the phone book. I asked how many street numbers there were in the square. Thirteen. With a little patience, I would surely end up finding out which one was hers.

Later on, I left my room and called directory enquiries again. No Dr Divoire in Fossombronne-la-Forêt. I walked, limping slightly, as far as the small bookshop at the beginning of Boulevard Jourdan. I bought a Michelin map of Loir-et-Cher. I turned around and walked towards Babel Café. My leg hurt. I sat at one of the tables on the indoor terrace. I was surprised when I saw on the clock that it was only seven in the evening. I was filled with sadness that

Hélène Navachine had left. I wanted to talk to someone. Should I walk up to Geneviève Dalame's building, a little further down the road? But she would be with Dr Bouvière, unless he was still in Pigalle. You have to let people live their lives. And really, I wasn't going to call at Geneviève Dalame's place unannounced…So I unfolded the Michelin map and spent a long time poring over Fossombronne—it was really important to me, and it made me forget my loneliness. Square de l'Alboni. Fossombronne-la-Forêt. I was about to learn something important about myself that would perhaps change the course of my life.

ON THE QUAY at the beginning of Rue de l'Alboni were two cafés facing each other. The busier was the one on the right, which sold cigarettes and newspapers. I ended up asking the boss if he knew a certain Jacqueline Beausergent. No, the name didn't ring a bell. A blonde woman who lived in the area. She'd had a car accident. No, he didn't think so, but perhaps I could try at the big garage, further along the quay, before the Trocadéro Gardens, the one that specialised in American cars. They had a lot of clients in the area. She had injuries on her face? That kind of thing would stand out. Go and ask at the garage. He wasn't surprised by my question and he had replied in a courteous, slightly weary voice, but I regretted having said Jacqueline Beausergent's name in front of him. You have to let others approach at their own pace. No sudden movements. Remain still and silent and blend into the background. I always sat at the most secluded table. And I waited. I was the type of person who would stop at the edge of a pool at dusk and allow my eyes to adjust to the darkness until I could see all the agitation beneath the surface of the still water. Going around the neighbouring streets in the area, I became more and more convinced that I would be able to find her without asking anyone anything. I had to tread carefully in this zone. It had taken me a long time to gain access to it. All my journeys across Paris, the travels during my childhood from the Left Bank to the Bois de Vincennes and the Bois de Boulogne, from south to north, the meetings with my father, and my own wanderings over the years, all of it had led me to this neighbourhood on the side of a hill, right by the Seine, a neighbourhood you could characterise simply as 'residential' or 'nondescript'. In a letter dated some fifteen years ago, but which I received only yesterday, someone had arranged to meet me here. But it wasn't too late: there was still someone waiting for me behind one of these windows, all identical, on façades of apartment buildings that all looked the same.

*

One morning when I was sitting in the café on the right, at the corner of the quay and Rue de l'Alboni, two men came in and sat at the counter. I recognised the huge brown-haired man straightaway. He was wearing the same dark coat he'd worn on the night of the accident and when I left the Mirabeau Clinic.

I tried to keep calm. He hadn't noticed me. I could see both of them from behind, sitting at the counter. They were speaking quietly. The other man was taking notes in a pad, nodding from time to time as he listened to the huge brown-haired man. I was at a table quite close to the counter, but I didn't catch a word of what they said. Why had he seemed like a 'huge brown-haired man' the first time I'd seen him, when the woman and I were side by side on the sofa in the lobby and he'd walked towards us? The shock of the accident must have blurred my vision. And the other day, leaving the clinic, I still wasn't quite feeling myself. In fact, he had a certain elegance, but his low hairline and features had something brutal about them and reminded me of an American actor whose name I've forgotten.

I hesitated for a few moments. But I couldn't let the chance slip by. I got up and propped my elbows on the counter next to him. He half-turned his back to me and I leaned over to attract his attention. It was the other man who noticed that I wanted to talk to him. He tapped him on the shoulder and pointed at me. He turned to face me. I remained silent, but I don't think it was only out of timidity. I was trying to find the right words, hoping he would recognise me. But he looked surprised and annoyed.

'Good to see you again,' I said and held out my hand.

He shook it distractedly. 'Have we met before?' he asked, frowning.

'The last time was not far from here. At the Mirabeau Clinic.'

The other man stared at me coldly, too. 'Excuse me? I don't understand…' There was a trace of a smile on his lips.

'Where did you say?'

'The Mirabeau Clinic.'

'You must be mistaken.'

He looked me up and down, perhaps to gauge the threat I posed. He noticed my left shoe. I had widened the split in my moccasin—for the bandage. If I remember correctly, I had even cut away most of the leather to free my ankle and I wore it without a sock, like the bandages that thoroughbreds sometimes have wrapped around their ankles because of their fragility.

'It was the accident,' I said. But he didn't seem to understand. 'Yes, the accident the other night...Place des Pyramides...' He looked at me in silence. I got the impression he was taunting me. 'Speaking of which,' I said, 'I wanted to know if there's been any news from Jacqueline Beausergent...'

He put a cigarette in his mouth and the other man held out a lighter, without taking his eyes off me either. 'I don't understand a word of what you're saying, sir.' His tone was quite contemptuous, the way you'd address a homeless person or a drunk.

The boss of the café came over, surprised at the way I was behaving with a customer he seemed to respect—even fear. And it was true that there was something unsettling about this man's face and his low, dark hairline. And even the tone of his slightly hoarse voice. But he didn't scare me. Ever since I was a child, I'd seen so many strange men in my father's company...This man was no more fearsome than the others.

'I also wanted to let you know...I really don't need all this money.' And from the inside pocket of my sheepskin jacket I took out the large wad of notes he had given me when I left the Mirabeau Clinic and which I was still carrying with me. He gave a disdainful flick of the hand.

'Sorry, sir…That's quite enough.' Then he turned back to the man next to him. They continued their conversation in hushed tones, ignoring my presence. I went and sat back down at my table. Behind the counter, the boss stared at me, shaking his head as if to say that my behaviour had been inappropriate and that I had got off lightly. Why? I would have loved to know.

When they left the café, they didn't even glance over at me. Through the window, I watched them walk along the pavement next to the quay. I thought about following them. No, it was better not to rush things. And already I regretted having lost my composure in front of him. I ought to have stayed in my corner, without attracting his attention, and waited until he left to follow him. And then find out who he was and see if he could lead me to her. But having wasted this chance, I feared I had burned my bridges.

From behind the counter, the boss continued to look at me somewhat disapprovingly.

'I must have mistaken him for someone else,' I said.

'Do you know that man's name?' He seemed reluctant and hesitated a moment, then he blurted it out, as if despite himself.

'Solière.'

He said that I was lucky Solière hadn't taken offence at my bad manners. What bad manners? A car had knocked me over the other night and I was simply trying to identify and find the driver. Was that unreasonable of me? I think I managed to convince him.

'I understand...' He smiled.

'And who exactly is this Solière?' I asked.

His smile broadened. My question seemed to amuse him. 'He's no choirboy,' he said. 'No, he's no choirboy...' I could tell from his evasive tone that I wouldn't get any more out of him.

'Does he live in the neighbourhood?'

'He used to live around here, but not any more, I don't think,' he said.

'And do you know if he's married?'

'I couldn't tell you.'

Other customers arrived and interrupted our conversation. He had forgotten about me, anyway. It was presumptuous of me to think he gave a second thought to my exchange with Solière. Customers come and go, they whisper among themselves. There's shouting too. Sometimes, very late at night, the police have to be called. In all the commotion, the comings and goings, a few faces, a few names stand out. But not for very long.

*

I thought that, with a little luck, the car would turn up again, parked somewhere in the neighbourhood. I walked up to the big garage on the quay and asked the petrol-pump assistant if, among his customers, he knew of a blonde woman who had recently been in a car accident and had injuries to her face. She drove a sea-green Fiat. He thought about it for a moment. No, he couldn't help me. There was so much traffic on the quay…You'd think it was a motorway. He didn't even notice his customers' faces anymore. Far too many customers. And Fiats. And so many blonde women… Then I ended up further down the quay, in the Trocadéro Gardens. I thought it was the first time I'd walked in the gardens, but in front of the aquarium building, a vague childhood memory came back to me. I bought a ticket and went in. I stayed a long time watching the fish behind the glass. Their phosphorescent colours reminded me of something. Someone had brought me here, but I couldn't say exactly when. Before Biarritz? Between Biarritz and Jouy-en-Josas?

Or was it shortly after I returned to Paris, just before I had quite reached the age of reason?

I thought it was around the same time as when I was hit by the van outside the school. And then, contemplating the fish in silence, I remembered the café boss's reply when I asked him who exactly the man named Solière was: 'He's no choirboy.' I had been a choirboy, at one point in my life. It was not something I ever thought about, and the memory of it came back to me suddenly. It was at midnight mass in a village church. Although I searched through my memory, it could only have been Fossombronne-la-Forêt, where the school and the convent were, as well as a certain Dr Divoire, who directory enquiries had told me was no longer in the phone book. She was the only one who could have taken me to midnight mass and to the Trocadéro aquarium. Under the van's tarpaulin, she held my hand and leaned over me.

The memory was far more distinct in this silent space, illuminated by the light of the tanks. Returning from midnight mass, along a small street, up to the front door of the house, someone was holding my hand. It was the same person. And I had come here during the same period, I had contemplated the same multicoloured fish gliding by behind the glass in silence. I wouldn't have been surprised to hear footsteps behind me and to see her coming towards me when I turned around, as if all those years amounted to nothing. What's more, we made the journey from Fossombronne-la-Forêt to Paris in the same car as the one that hit me on Place des Pyramides, a sea-green car. It had never stopped driving around the streets of Paris at night, looking for me.

When I left the aquarium, I was overwhelmed by the cold. Along the paths and lawns of the gardens, there were little piles of snow. The sky was a limpid blue. I felt I could see clearly for the first time in my life. This blue, against which the Palais de Chaillot was sharply silhouetted, this bracing cold after years and years of torpor…The accident the other night had come at the right time. I needed a shock to wake me out of my lethargy. I couldn't carry on walking around in fog. And it happened a few months before I turned twenty-one. What a strange coincidence. I'd been saved just in time. That accident would probably be one of the most defining events of my life. A return to order.

The school and the van with a tarpaulin: it was the first time I revisited the past. It was triggered by the shock of the accident the other night. Until that point I had lived from one day to the next. I'd been driving on a road covered with black ice in what could have been described as zero-visibility conditions. I'd had to avoid looking back. Perhaps I'd turned onto a bridge that was too narrow. It was impossible to turn around. One glance in the rear-view mirror and I would have been consumed by vertigo. But now I could look back over those unfortunate years without fear. It was as though someone other than myself had a bird's eye view of my life, or that I was looking at my own X-ray against a backlit screen. Everything was so clear, the lines so precise and pure…Only the essential elements were left: the van, the face leaning over me under the tarpaulin, ether, midnight mass and the walk home up to the front gate of the house where her room was on the first floor, at the end of the corridor.

I FOUND A hotel past the Pont de Bir-Hakeim on a small avenue that ran onto the quay. After three days, I no longer wanted to go back to my room in Porte d'Orléans, so I took a room at the Hôtel Fremiet, and wondered who the other guests were. It was a more comfortable room than the one on Rue de la Voie-Verte, with a telephone and even its own bathroom. But I could afford this luxury thanks to the money the man named Solière had given me, which he had turned down when I tried to give it back. That was his bad luck. It was foolish of me to have any scruples about it. After all, he was no choirboy.

At night, in my room, I decided never to return to Rue de la Voie-Verte. I had taken some clothes and the navy-blue cardboard box in which I kept my old papers. I had to face the facts: there was no trace of me left there. Far from making me sad, the thought gave me courage for the future. A weight had been lifted.

I used to get back late to the hotel. I'd eat dinner in a large restaurant, past the steps from the bridge and the entrance to the metro station. I still remember the name: La Closerie de Passy. It wasn't very busy. Some nights I would find myself alone with the manager, a woman with short brown hair, and the waiter, who wore a white naval jacket. Every time I went, I hoped Jacqueline Beausergent would come in and walk over to the bar like the two or three people who sat and talked with the manager. I always chose the closest table to the entrance. I would stand up and walk towards her. I had already decided what I would say to her: 'We were both in an accident at Place des Pyramides...' Seeing me walk would be enough. The split moccasin, the bandage... At the Hôtel Fremiet, the man at reception had looked me over with a frown. The bloodstain on my old sheepskin jacket was still there. He didn't seem to trust me. I paid a fortnight's rent in advance.

But the manager of La Closerie de Passy wasn't fazed by my bandage and the bloodstain on my old sheepskin jacket. Apparently she had seen it all before, in neighbourhoods that weren't as quiet as this one. Next to the bar was a parrot in a large yellow cage. Decades later, I was leafing through a magazine from the time and, on the last page, there were advertisements for restaurants. One of them jumped out at me: 'La Closerie de Passy and its parrot, Pépère. Open seven days a week.' A seemingly harmless phrase, but it made my heart race. One night, I was feeling so lonely that I went to sit at the bar with the others and I sensed that the manager took pity on me because of my stained sheepskin jacket, my bandage, and because I was so thin. She advised me to drink some Viandox. When I asked her a question about the parrot she said, 'You can teach him a sentence if you like.' So I thought about it and ended up saying as clearly as possible, '*I'm looking for a sea-green Fiat car.*' It didn't take long to teach it to him. His way of saying it was more concise and efficient: '*sea-green Fiat*', and his voice was more shrill and imperious than mine.

La Closerie de Passy isn't there anymore and one night last summer when I was going along Boulevard Delessert in a taxi, it looked as if there was a bank in its place. But parrots live to a very old age. Perhaps this one, after thirty years, is still repeating my phrase in another neighbourhood of Paris and in the commotion of another café, without anyone understanding it or really paying any attention. Nowadays only parrots remain faithful to the past.

*

I used to prolong my dinner at La Closerie de Passy as long as possible. At around ten o'clock the manager and her friends would sit at a table at the back, near the bar and near Pépère's yellow cage. They would begin playing cards. She even invited me to join them one night. But it was time for me to continue my search. SEA-GREEN FIAT.

I thought that by walking around the streets of the neighbourhood towards midnight, I might be lucky enough to come across the car parked somewhere. Jacqueline Beausergent would surely be home at that time. It seemed more likely that I would eventually find THE SEA-GREEN FIAT at night rather than during the day.

The streets were silent, the cold went straight through me. Of course, now and again, I was frightened that a police van doing its rounds would stop alongside me and ask to see my papers. My bloodstained sheepskin jacket and the bandage visible through my split moccasin must have made me look like a prowler. And I was still a few months shy of twenty-one. But, luckily, on those particular nights no police van stopped to drive me to the nearest police station or to the large, dingy buildings of the juvenile police department on the banks of the Seine.

I started at Square de l'Alboni. No sea-green Fiat among the cars parked there, on either side of the road. I was convinced that she could never find a spot out the front of her apartment, that she would drive around for ages in the neighbourhood looking for somewhere to park. No doubt she ended up quite far away. Unless her car was in a garage. There was one near her place, on Boulevard Delessert. I went in one night. There was a man at the back, in a sort of glass-walled office. He saw me from afar. As I pushed the door open, he stood up and I got the feeling that he was on the defensive. At that moment I regretted not wearing a new coat. As soon as I started talking, he relaxed. A car had knocked me over the other night and I was almost certain that the driver lived in the area. I hadn't heard anything from the driver and I wanted to get in contact. Incidentally, it was a female driver. Yes, Square de l'Alboni. A sea-green Fiat. The woman had some injuries on her face and the Fiat was a bit damaged.

He consulted a large register that was already lying open on his desk. He put his index finger to his lower lip and slowly turned the pages. It was a gesture my father often made while examining mysterious files at the Corona or the Ruc-Univers. 'You did say a sea-green Fiat?' He held his index finger in the middle of the page, pointing at something. My heart was pounding. Actually there was a sea-green Fiat, licence plate…He lifted his head and considered me with the solemnity of a doctor in a consultation.

'The car belongs to a certain Solière,' he said. 'I have his address.'

'Does he live on Square de l'Alboni?'

'No, not at all.' He frowned as if thinking twice about giving me his address.

'You said it was a woman. Are you sure it's the same car?' So I took him back through the events of that night: she and I going in the police van with Solière, the Hôtel-Dieu, the Mirabeau Clinic, and Solière again, waiting for me in the foyer when I left the clinic. I didn't want to tell him about my last encounter with him in the café, when he pretended not to recognise me.

'He lives at 4 Avenue Albert-de-Mun,' he said. 'But he's not one of our regular clients. It was the first time he's been here.' I asked him where Avenue Albert-de-Mun was. Over that way. It runs along Trocadéro Gardens. Near the aquarium? A bit further on. An avenue that runs down towards the quay. The windscreen and one of the headlights had been replaced, but someone had come to collect the car before the repairs were finished. Solière himself? He couldn't tell me, he was away that day. He would ask his business partner. From time to time he glanced at my split moccasin and bandage. 'You've pressed charges, haven't you?' His tone was reprimanding but almost affectionate, like the pharmacist's the other day. Against whom? The only charges I could press were against myself. Up until then my life had been chaotic. The accident was going to bring an end to all the years of confusion and uncertainty. It was time.

'And is there any sign of a Madame Solière?' I asked. 'Or a Jacqueline Beausergent? Not in the register, in any case. A blonde woman, with injuries on her face? You've never seen her around the neighbourhood?'

He shrugged his shoulders. 'I'm always in the office, you know. Apart from when I go home, to Vanves. Are you sure she was driving?'

I was sure. That night, we'd sat next to each other for a long time on the sofa in the hotel lobby, before the man named Solière had walked towards us and we'd got in the police van. I could go and check at the hotel on Place des

Pyramides. There must have been a witness. But I didn't need a witness. All I needed was to find this woman to clear things up with her, that was all.

'Go and see at Avenue-Albert-de-Mun,' he said. 'If they happen to bring the Fiat back, I'll let you know. Where can I reach you?' I gave him the address of the Hôtel Fremiet. After all, he didn't mean me any harm.

It was around midnight and I walked to the Trocadéro Gardens. Solière. I repeated the name...I had kept an old address book of my father's, which should be in the navy-blue cardboard box. I would check under the letter S.

I walked along the pathway to the aquarium. Yes, Avenue Albert-de-Mun ran down towards the Seine and along the Trocadéro Gardens. Number 4 was one of two apartment buildings before the quay. It stood on the corner of a small street and there was a terrace on the top floor. No light at any of the windows. The building looked abandoned. From time to time a car went past on the quay. I walked up to the glass doorway, but I didn't dare go in. Any concierge, seeing me dressed as I was, and at that hour, would be sure to call the police. Was there a concierge? And what floor did this Solière live on? I remained standing on the pavement, next to the gardens, without taking my eyes off the façade. It was in there, on one of the floors, that I was to learn something important about my life. It seemed to me that one afternoon in my childhood, after leaving the aquarium, I had walked down this road, alongside the gardens. Four Avenue Albert-de-Mun. Still, I would check in my father's old notebook to see if the address appeared on any of the pages, preceded by a name, Solière or another name. Perhaps the village of Fossombronne-la-Forêt was mentioned. Sooner or later, I would find out what connected the two places. I must have made numerous journeys between Fossombronne-la-Forêt and Paris in the sea-green Fiat or in another older car that this Jacqueline Beausergent drove. The longer I contemplated the white façade, the more I felt that I had seen it before—a fleeting sensation like the fragments of a dream that slip away as you wake up, or light from the moon. In my room at Porte d'Orléans, I would never have imagined that this neighbourhood and the Avenue Albert-de-Mun would become a magnetic zone for me. Up until then, I lived on the fringes, in the suburbs of life, waiting for something. Even now in my dreams, I find myself back in these neighbourhoods where I'm lost among all the tall apartment buildings on the outskirts of Paris. I search in vain for my old room, the one from before the accident.

I walked down to the quay. No sea-green Fiat there either. I walked around the apartment block. Perhaps she was away. And how would I find Solière's phone number? Considering his demeanour in the café the other day, he didn't seem the type you'd find in the phone book.

*

The pharmacist on Rue Raynouard was kind enough to change my dressings a few times. He disinfected the cut with Mercurochrome and advised me not to walk so much and to find a more appropriate shoe than the split moccasin for my left foot. Each time I went, I promised to follow his advice. But I knew very well that I wouldn't change my shoes until I found the sea-green Fiat.

I tried to walk less than the previous days and I spent long afternoons in the Hôtel Fremiet. I thought about the past and the present. I had made a note of the names of the people living at 4 Avenue Albert-de-Mun who were in the phone book.

Boscher (J.): PASSY 13 51
Trocadéro Finance and Real Estate Co: PASSY 48 00

Destombe (J.): PASSY 03 97

Dupont (A.): PASSY 24 35

Goodwin (Mme C.): PASSY 41 48

Grunberg (A.): PASSY 05 00

McLachlan (G. V.): PASSY 04 38

No Solière. I called each of the numbers and asked to speak to a Monsieur Solière or a Mademoiselle Jacqueline Beausergent, but neither of the names seemed to ring a bell for any of the people I spoke to. There was no answer from the Trocadéro Finance and Real Estate Company. So perhaps that was the right number.

My father's address book was there in the navy-blue cardboard box. He'd forgotten it on the table at a café one night and I'd slipped it into my pocket. He never mentioned it during our subsequent meetings. Losing it was evidently not a problem for him, or perhaps he couldn't imagine that I would take it. During the few months before he disappeared into the fog around Montrouge I don't think any of those names were of much use to him any longer. No Solière under the letter S. And no mention of Fossombronne-la-Forêt among the addresses.

Some nights, I wondered if this search was meaningless

and I questioned why I had embarked upon it. Was it naïve of me? Very early on, perhaps even before adolescence, I had the feeling that I came from nothing. I remembered a rainy afternoon in the Latin Quarter, a fellow with a jawline beard in a grey trench coat was handing out leaflets. It was a questionnaire for a study about young people. The questions seemed strange to me: What family structure did you grow up in? I answered: none. Do you have a strong image of your mother and father? I answered: nebulous. Do you think you are a good son (or daughter)? I answered: I have never been a son. In the studies you have undertaken, have you endeavoured to keep your parents' respect and to conform to your social group? No studies. No parents. No social group. Would you prefer to be part of the revolution or contemplate a beautiful landscape? Contemplate a beautiful landscape. Which do you prefer? The depth of torment or the lightness of happiness? The lightness of happiness. Do you want to change your life or rediscover a lost harmony? Rediscover a lost harmony. These two words were the stuff of dreams, but what could a lost harmony really consist of? In the room at the Hôtel Fremiet, I asked myself if I wasn't trying to discover, despite the obscurity of my origins and the chaos of my childhood, a fixed point, something reassuring, a landscape even, that would help me to regain my footing. There was perhaps a whole section of my life that I didn't know about, a solid foundation beneath the shifting sands. And I was relying on the sea-green Fiat and its driver to help me discover it.

*

I was having trouble sleeping. I was tempted to go and ask the pharmacist for one of the midnight-blue vials of ether I knew so well. But I stopped myself in time. It wasn't the moment to give in. I had to remain as lucid as possible. During those sleepless nights, what I regretted most was having left all my books in my room on Rue de la Voie-Verte. There weren't many bookshops in the area. I walked towards l'Étoile to find one. I bought some detective novels and an old second-hand book, the title of which intrigued me: *The Wonders of the Heavens*. To my great surprise, I couldn't bring myself to read detective novels anymore. But hardly had I opened *The Wonders of the Heavens*, which bore on its first page the words 'Night reading', than I realised just how much this book was going to mean to me. Nebula. The Milky Way. The Sidereal World. The Northern Constellations. The Zodiac, Distant

Universes…As I read through the chapters, I no longer even knew why I was lying on that bed in that hotel room. I had forgotten where I was, which country, which city, and none of it mattered anymore. No drug, not ether or morphine or opium, could have given me that sense of calm, which gradually engulfed me. All I had to do was turn the pages. This 'night reading' should have been recommended to me a long time ago. It would have spared me much pointless suffering and many restless nights. The Milky Way. The Sidereal World. Finally, the horizon stretched out infinitely before me and I felt utterly content looking at stars from afar and trying to make out all the variable, temporary, extinguished or faded stars. I was nothing in this infinity, but I could finally breathe.

Was it the influence of my reading? When I walked around the neighbourhood at night, I continued to feel a sense of fulfilment. All my anxiety was gone. I had been freed from some kind of suffocating restraint. My leg didn't hurt anymore. The bandage had come undone and was dangling from my shoe. The wound was healing. The neighbourhood took on an aspect that was different from when I first arrived. For a few nights the sky was so clear that I could see more stars than ever before. Or perhaps I hadn't noticed them until then. But now I had read *The Wonders of the Heavens*.

My walks often led to the Trocadéro esplanade. At least one could breathe the ocean air there. This zone now seemed to be crisscrossed by large avenues that one could reach from the Seine via gardens, sequences of stairways and walkways that looked like country paths. The light from the streetlamps was more and more dazzling. I was surprised that there were no cars parked along the kerb. Every avenue was deserted, and it would be easy for me to spot the sea-green Fiat from a distance. Perhaps parking in the area had been prohibited for the past few nights. They had decided that from then on the neighbourhood would be what they called a 'blue zone'. And I was the only pedestrian. Had a curfew been brought in which forbade people from going out after eleven o'clock at night? But I didn't care: it was as if I had a special pass in the pocket of my sheepskin jacket, which exempted me from police checks.

One night, a dog followed me from Pont de l'Alma to the Trocadéro esplanade. It was the same black colouring and the same breed as the one that had been hit by a car in my childhood. I walked up the avenue on the right-hand side. At first, the dog stayed about ten metres behind me and then gradually it came closer. By the time we reached the railings of the Galliera Gardens, we were walking side by side. I don't know where I'd read—perhaps in a footnote in *The Wonders of the Heavens*—that at certain hours of the night, you can slip into a parallel world: an empty apartment where the light wasn't switched off, even a small dead-end street. It's where you find objects lost long ago: a lucky charm, a letter, an umbrella, a key, and cats, dogs and horses that were lost over the course of your life. I thought that dog was the one from Rue du Docteur-Kurzenne.

It wore a red leather collar with a metal tag and, when I bent down, I saw a phone number engraved on it. With a collar, you'd think twice about taking it to the pound. As for me, I still kept an old, out-of-date passport in the inside pocket of my sheepskin jacket. I had fudged the date of birth to make myself older, and so it looked like I was twenty-one. For the past few nights, however, I no longer feared police checks. Reading *The Wonders of the Heavens* had lifted my spirits. From then on, I considered things from high above.

The dog walked in front of me. At first, it looked around to check that I was following, and then it walked at a steady pace, certain I would follow. I walked at the same slow pace as the dog. Nothing interrupted the silence. Grass seemed to be growing in between the cobblestones. Time had ceased.

It must have been what Bouvière called the 'eternal return'. The façades of buildings, the trees, the glimmer of the street-lamps took on an intensity that I had never seen in them before.

The dog hesitated for a moment when I turned onto the Trocadéro esplanade. It seemed to want to continue straight ahead. It ended up following me. I paused for a while to look at the gardens below, the big pool where the water appeared phosphorescent and, beyond the Seine, the apartment buildings along the quays and around the Champ-de-Mars.

I thought of my father. I imagined him over there, in a room somewhere, or in a café, just before closing time, sitting alone under the neon lights, looking through his files. Perhaps there was still a chance I would find him. After all, time had been abolished, given that this dog had emerged from the depths of the past, from Rue du Docteur-Kurzenne. I watched the dog move away from me, as though it would soon have to leave me or it might miss another engagement. I followed. It walked alongside the façade of the Musée de l'Homme and started down Rue Vineuse. I'd never been down this road. If the dog was leading me there, it wasn't by chance. I had the feeling of both arriving at my destination and returning to familiar ground. But there was no light from the windows and I walked along in half-darkness. I moved closer to the dog so I wouldn't lose sight of it. Silence surrounded us. I could hear the sound of my footsteps. The road turned almost at a right angle and I thought it would come out near La Closerie de Passy where, at that hour, the parrot in its cage would be repeating, *Sea-green Fiat, sea-green Fiat*, for no reason, while the manager and her friends played cards. After the angle in the road, an unlit sign. A restaurant or, rather, a bar, closed. It was Sunday. What an odd place for a bar: the pale wooden shopfront and sign would have been better suited to the Champs-Élysées or Pigalle.

I stopped for a moment and tried to decipher the sign above the entrance: Vol de Nuit. Then I looked ahead for the dog. I couldn't see it. I hurried to catch up. But there was no trace of it. I ran and came out at the crossroads on Boulevard Delessert. The streetlamps were so bright they made me squint. No dog to be seen, not on the pavement that ran downhill, not on the other side of the boulevard, not opposite me near the little metro station and the steps that led down to the Seine. The light was white, the brightness of the northern lights: the black dog would have been visible from a distance. But it had disappeared. I felt a sensation of emptiness with which I was familiar and which I had forgotten for a few days, thanks to the calming effect of reading *The Wonders of the Heavens*. I regretted not having made a note of the phone number on the dog's collar.

*

I slept badly that night. I dreamed of the dog that had sprung out of the past only to disappear again. In the morning, I was in good spirits and I was sure that neither the dog nor I were in danger of anything anymore. No car could ever knock us over again.

It was not quite seven o'clock. One of the cafés on the quay was open, the one where I had come across Solière. On that occasion, my father's old address book was stuffed into the pocket of my sheepskin jacket. I always kept something in my pockets: the copy of *The Wonders of the Heavens* or the Michelin map of Loir-et-Cher.

I sat at a table close to the bay window. Over on the other side of the bridge, metro carriages disappeared one after the other. I leafed through the address book. The names were in inks of different colours—blue, black, purple. The names in purple seemed to be the oldest and in more careful handwriting. A few of them had been crossed out. I noticed rather a lot of names, which, to my surprise, had addresses in the neighbourhood I was in at that moment. I kept the notebook and here is the transcription:

Yvan Schaposchnikoff, 1 Avenue Paul-Doumer
KLÉBER 73 46
Guy de Voisins, 23 Rue Raynouard JASMIN 33 18
Nick de Morgoli, 14 Square de l'Alboni
TROCADÉRO 65 81
Toddie Werner, 28 Rue Scheffer PASSY 90 90
Mary Tchernycheff, 30 Quai de Passy JASMIN 64 76
And again, 30 Quai de Passy: Alexis Moutafolo,
AUTEUIL 70 66

In the afternoon, out of curiosity, I went to some of these addresses. Again, the same pale façades with bay windows and large terraces, like 4 Avenue Albert-de-Mun. I assume these apartments were said to have 'modern comforts' and certain features: heated flooring, marble tiles instead of parquet, sliding doors, giving the impression of being on a stationary cruise ship in the middle of the ocean. And the void behind the luxury all too visible. I knew that since his childhood, my father had often lived in this type of building, and that he didn't pay the rent. In winter, in the empty rooms, the electricity would be cut off. He was one of those transients who were forever changing their identity, never settling anywhere, never leaving a trace. Yes, the type of person whose existence one would have trouble proving later on. It was useless to collect precise details: phone numbers, letters of the alphabet marking different stairwells in courtyards. That's why I felt discouraged the other night on Avenue Albert-de-Mun. If I went through the porte-cochère, it wouldn't lead anywhere. It was this, rather than the fear of being arrested for prowling, that held me back. I was conducting a search around streets where everything was an optical illusion. My task seemed as vain as that of a surveyor trying to draw up a plan in an empty space. But I said to myself: is it really beyond me to track down this Jacqueline Beausergent?

I REMEMBER THAT night I had taken a break from reading *The Wonders of the Heavens,* in the middle of a chapter on constellations of the southern hemisphere. I left the hotel without handing in my room key—there was no one at the reception desk. I wanted to buy a packet of cigarettes. The only *café-tabac* still open was on Place du Trocadéro.

From the quay, I climbed the steps and, after passing the little station, I thought I heard the rasping voice of the parrot from La Closerie repeating: *Sea-green Fiat, sea-green Fiat.* There was light at the window. They were still playing their card game. I was surprised by how warm the air was for a winter's night. It had been snowing over the previous few days and there were still patches of snow dotted around the gardens below, in front of the Musée de l'Homme.

While I was buying cigarettes at the bigger *café-tabac*, a group of tourists sat down at the tables on the terrace. I could hear their peals of laughter. I was surprised that tables had been put outside and for an instant I felt a kind of vertigo. I wondered if I hadn't perhaps confused the seasons. But no, the trees around the square had indeed lost their leaves and there would still be a long wait before summer came around again. I had been walking around for months and months in so much cold and fog that I no longer knew if the veil would ever be stripped away again. Was it really demanding too much from life to want to lie in the sun, drinking orangeade with a straw?

I remained awhile on the esplanade breathing in the ocean aïr. I thought about the black dog that had come to accompany me the other night, the dog that had come from so far away, across all these years…How stupid not to have kept the phone number.

I headed along Rue Vineuse, as I had the other night. It was still dark there. Perhaps there had been a power cut. I saw the bar or restaurant with its illuminated sign, but so faint that I could only just make out the dark mass of a car parked just before the turn in the road. When I got to it, my heart skipped a beat. It was the sea-green Fiat. It wasn't

really a surprise; I had never given up hope that I would find
it. I'd just had to be patient, that was all, and I felt I had huge
reserves of patience within me. Come rain or snow, I was
prepared to wait for hours in the street.

The bumper bar and one of the mudguards were
damaged. There were probably a lot of sea-green Fiats in
Paris, but this one certainly bore the signs of the accident. I
took my passport out of the pocket of my sheepskin jacket. It
contained the folded piece of paper that Solière had made
me sign. Yes, it was the same licence plate number.

I looked in through the window. A travel bag on the
back seat. I could have left a note under the windscreen
wiper, giving my name and the address of the Hôtel Fremiet.
But I wanted to get to the bottom of it there and then. The
car was parked right in front of the restaurant. So I pushed
the pale wooden door and went in.

Light fell from a wall lamp behind the bar, leaving the
few tables arranged along the walls on either side in darkness. And yet, I can see these walls clearly in my memory;
they are draped with very worn, red velvet that is ripped and
torn here and there, as though, long ago, the place had been
quite lavish, but no one went there anymore. Apart from me.
At first I thought it was well after closing time. A woman was

sitting at the bar wearing a dark brown coat. A young man, the size of a jockey and the look of one, was clearing the tables. He looked askance at me.

'What can I do for you?'

It would take too long to explain. I walked towards the bar and, instead of sitting on one of the stools, I stopped behind her. I put my hand on her shoulder. She turned around with a start. She stared at me, astonished. There was a large graze across her forehead, just above the eyebrows.

'Are you Jacqueline Beausergent?'

I was surprised by the detachment in my voice; I even had the impression that someone else had spoken for me. She gazed at me in silence. She lowered her eyes; they lingered on the stain on my sheepskin jacket, then lower down, on my shoe where the bandage was dangling out.

'We've already met at Place des Pyramides…'

My voice seemed even clearer and more detached. I was standing behind her.

'Yes…Yes…I remember very well. Place des Pyramides.'

Without looking away, she gave a slightly wry smile, the same—it seemed—as the other night, in the police van.

'Why don't we sit down…'

She gestured to the table closest to the bar, which was

still covered with a white tablecloth. We sat opposite each other. She put her glass down on the tablecloth. I wondered what kind of alcohol it contained.

'You should drink something,' she said. 'Something to warm you up. You're very pale.'

She said the words with great seriousness and even a kind of solemn affection that no one had ever shown towards me until then. I felt embarrassed.

'Have a margarita like me.'

The jockey brought me a margarita and then disappeared through a glass door behind the bar.

'I didn't know you'd left the clinic,' she said. 'I've been away from Paris for a few weeks…I'd planned on finding out how you were.'

It seems to me now, after decades, that it was very gloomy in that place where we'd found ourselves sitting face to face. We were in darkness, like in an eye clinic where they hold up lenses of different strengths in front of your eyes so that eventually you can make out the letters, over there on the backlit screen.

'You should have stayed longer at the clinic…Did you escape?' She smiled again. Stayed longer? I didn't understand. The letters were still very blurry on the screen.

'They told me to leave,' I said. 'A Mr Solière came to find me.'

She seemed surprised. She shrugged. 'He didn't tell me about it. I think he was afraid of you.'

Afraid of me? I would never have imagined frightening anyone.

'You struck him as quite strange. He's not used to people like you.'

She seemed embarrassed. I didn't venture to ask what it was exactly that constituted my strangeness in the eyes of this Solière.

'I came to see you two or three times at the clinic. Unfortunately, it was always when you were asleep.'

I hadn't been told about these visits. Suddenly, a doubt crossed my mind.

'Did I stay long at the clinic?'

'About ten days. It was Mr Solière's idea to have you taken there. They wouldn't have been able to keep you at the Hôtel-Dieu in the state you were in.'

'That bad?'

'They thought you had taken toxic substances.'

She said these last words very carefully. I don't believe I had ever heard anyone speak to me so calmly, with such a soft voice. Listening to her produced the same soothing effect as reading *The Wonders of the Heavens*. I couldn't take my eyes off the large graze across her forehead, just above her eyebrows. Her clear eyes, her shoulder-length chestnut hair, the upturned collar of her coat...Because of the late hour and the darkness around us, she looked just as she had in the police van the other night.

She ran her index finger along the graze above her eyebrows and, again, she gave her wry smile.

'For a first meeting,' she said, 'it was a bit of a shock.'

She stared straight into my eyes in silence, as if she was trying to read my thoughts—I had never before experienced such attentiveness.

'I thought you purposely chose that moment to cross Place des Pyramides...'

That's not what I thought. I had always resisted the pull of vertigo. I would never have been capable of throwing myself into the void from the top of a bridge or from a window. Or even under a car, as she seemed to believe. For me, at the last moment, life was always the stronger force.

'I don't think you were quite yourself...'

She glanced again at my sheepskin jacket and the split moccasin on my left foot. I had tried my best to reapply the bandage, but I mustn't have looked very prepossessing. I apologised for my appearance. Yes, I was quite keen to look human again.

She said in a quiet voice, 'All you have to do is change your sheepskin jacket. And perhaps your shoes, too.'

I felt more and more at ease. I confessed that I had spent the last few weeks trying to find her. It wasn't easy with a street name but no number. So I had looked all over the neighbourhood for her sea-green Fiat.

'Sea-green?'

She seemed intrigued by this adjective, but that was how it had been described on the report that Solière made me sign. A report? She wasn't aware of any report. It was still in the inside pocket of my sheepskin jacket, so I showed it to her. She read it, frowning.

'I'm not surprised. He's always been wary.'

'He also gave me some money.'

'He's a generous man,' she said.

I wanted to know what the link was between her and Solière. 'Do you live on Square de l'Alboni?'

'No. It's the address of one of Monsieur Solière's offices.'

Whenever she said his name, it was inflected with a certain respect.

'And Avenue Albert-de-Mun?' To my great shame, I sounded like a cop who throws in an unexpected question to unnerve a suspect.

'It's one of Monsieur Solière's apartments.' She wasn't fazed in the slightest. 'How do you know about this address?' she asked.

I told her that I had met Solière the other day in a café and that he had pretended not to recognise me.

'He's very distrustful, you know. He always thinks people are after him. He has a lot of lawyers.'

'He's your boss?'

I immediately regretted asking the question.

'I've worked for him for two years.' She answered calmly, as if it were an entirely ordinary question. And it was, surely. Why search for mystery where there is none?

'That night, I was meeting Monsieur Solière at Place des Pyramides in the lobby of the Hôtel Régina. And then, just as I arrived, we had our…accident.' She hesitated before saying the word. She looked at my left hand. When the car knocked me down, I grazed the back of it. But it was almost healed. I hadn't put a dressing on it.

'Then if I've understood correctly, Monsieur Solière arrived at the right moment?'

He had walked towards us slowly that night, in his dark coat. I even wonder if he had a cigarette at the corner of his mouth. And this girl had a meeting with him in the lobby of the hotel…I also had meetings with my father in hotel lobbies, which all looked the same and where the marble, the chandeliers, the wood engravings and the sofas were all fake. It's the same precarious situation as being in a railway station waiting room between catching two trains, or in a police station before an interrogation.

'It seems he's no choirboy,' I said.

'Who?'

'Solière.'

For the first time, she seemed embarrassed.

'What does he do for a living?'

'Business.'

She lowered her head as if I might be shocked by this response.

'And you're his secretary?'

'Sort of, I suppose…But only part-time.'

There under the light of the wall lamp, she seemed younger than in the police van. It must have been the fur coat that made her seem older the other night. And besides, after the shock, I didn't have my wits about me.

That night, I thought she was blonde.

'And the work isn't too complicated?'

I really wanted to know everything. Time was running out. At that hour, they were perhaps about to close the restaurant.

'When I came to Paris, I studied nursing,' she said, and started speaking more and more quickly as if she was in a hurry to explain it all to me. 'And then I started work… home nursing…I met Monsieur Solière…'

I wasn't listening anymore. I asked her how old she was. Twenty-six. So she was a few years older than me. But it was unlikely that she was the woman from Fossombronne-la-Forêt. I tried to remember the face of the woman or girl who had climbed into the van and held my hand.

'During my childhood, I had an accident that was similar to the one the other night. I was leaving school…'

As I told her the story, I spoke more and more quickly, too, the words tumbling out. We were like two people allowed a few minutes together in the visiting room of a prison and who wouldn't have enough time to tell each other everything.

'I thought the girl in the van was you.'

She burst out laughing.

'But that's impossible. I was twelve years old then.'

An entire episode of my life, the face of someone who must have loved me, a house, all of it tipped into oblivion, into the unknown, forever.

'A place called Fossombronne-la-Forêt...A Dr Divoire.' I thought I had said it under my breath, to myself.

'I know that name,' she said. 'It's in Sologne. I was born around there.'

I took the Michelin map of the Loir-et-Cher from the pocket of my sheepskin jacket, where I had kept it for several days. I unfolded it on the tablecloth. She seemed apprehensive.

'Where were you born?' I asked.

'La Versanne.'

I leaned over the map. The light from the wall lamp wasn't strong enough for me to make out all the names of the villages in such tiny print.

She craned her neck to look, too. Our foreheads were almost touching.

'Try to find Blois,' she said. 'Slightly to the right you have Chambord. Below there's the Boulogne forest. And Bracieux...and, to the right, La Versanne.'

It was easy to find my bearings with the forest marked

in green. There it was. I'd found La Versanne.

'Do you think it's far from Fossombronne?'

'About twenty kilometres.'

The first time I'd discovered it on the map, I should have underlined the name Fossombronne-la-Forêt in red ink. Now I'd lost it.

'It's on the road to Milançay,' she said.

I looked for the road to Milançay. Now I was managing to read the names of the villages: Fontaines-en-Sologne, Montgiron, Marcheval...

'If you really want to, I could show you around the area one day,' she said, staring at me with a perplexed look.

I leaned over the map again.

'We'd still have to find the route from La Versanne to Fossombronne.'

I buried myself in the map again, tracing departmental roads, heading from village to village at random: Le Plessis, Tréfontaine, Boizardiaire, La Viorne...At the end of a little winding road, I read: FOSSOMBRONNE-LA-FORÊT.

'And what if we went there tonight?'

She thought about it for a moment, as if my suggestion seemed perfectly natural. 'Not tonight, I'm too tired.'

I said that I was joking, but I wasn't sure. I couldn't tear my eyes from the names of all the hamlets, forests and little lakes. I wanted to merge with the landscape. Already at that time, I was convinced that a man without a landscape was thoroughly diminished. An invalid of sorts. I had become aware of it when I was very young, in Paris, when my dog died and I didn't know where to bury him. No field. No village. No land of our own. Not even a garden. I folded up the map and stuffed it into my pocket.

'Do you live with Solière?'

'Not at all. I just take care of his offices and his apartment when he's away from Paris. He travels a lot for business.'

It was funny; my father used to travel a lot for business as well and, despite all the meetings he arranged with me in increasingly distant hotel lobbies and cafés, I had never understood what line of business he was in. The same as Solière's?

'Do you come to this bar often?' I asked.

'No, not often. It's the only place open late in the area.'

I remarked that there weren't many customers, but she told me they came much later at night. A strange clientele, she said. And yet, in my memory, the place seems abandoned. It's as if she and I had broken in that night. There we are opposite each other and I can hear some of that muffled music played after the curfew hour—music which you can dance to and live a few moments of stolen happiness.

'Don't you think that after the shock of our first encounter, we should get to know each other better?'

She said this in a soft voice, but with clear, precise enunciation. I had read that in Touraine that they spoke the purest French. But listening to her, I wondered if it wasn't actually in Sologne, around La Versanne and Fossombronne-la-Forêt. She laid her hand on mine, my left hand where the cut was healing without a dressing.

*

Out in the street, a veil had been stripped away. The bonnet of the car was gleaming in the moonlight. I wondered if it was a mirage or the effect of the alcohol I'd drunk. I tapped on the car near the bonnet to make sure I wasn't dreaming.

'One day I'll have to get all that repaired,' she said, gesturing to the bumper and the damaged mudguard.

I confessed that it was at a garage that I'd been tipped off about her car.

'You've given yourself a lot of trouble for nothing,' she said. 'It's been parked in front of my place for the last three weeks. I live at 2 Square Léon-Guillot in the fifteenth arrondissement.'

So it turned out that we didn't live that far from each other. Porte d'Orléans. Porte de Vanves. With a little luck we might have come across each other there, in that hinterland. That would have simplified things. We were both from the same world.

I sat on the bonnet.

'Well, if you're going back to the fifteenth, I'd be glad of a lift home…'

But no. She said that she had to sleep at Solière's apartment that night, on Avenue Albert-de-Mun, and stay there for a while so that it wouldn't be empty while he was away. Solière had gone to Geneva and Madrid on business.

'If I understand correctly, you're employed as a caretaker and night watcher?'

'Sort of, I suppose.'

She opened the right-hand door for me to get into the car. After all those days and all these nights spent wandering around the neighbourhood, it seemed natural. I was even convinced that I had already lived that moment in a dream.

It was suddenly very cold, a dry cold that added a sharpness and clarity to everything around us: the white light of the streetlamps, the red traffic lights, the new façades of the buildings. In the silence, I thought I heard the steady footsteps of someone approaching.

She squeezed my wrist, just like the other night in the police van.

'Are you feeling better?' she asked.

Place du Trocadéro was much more vast and deserted than usual because of the moonlight. Crossing it would take forever, and the slowness felt good. I was sure that, if I looked at the black windows, I would be able to penetrate the darkness of the apartments, as if I could perceive infrared and ultraviolet light. But I didn't have to go to the trouble. I just had to let myself glide down the hill I had walked up the other night with the dog.

'I also tried to find you,' she said, 'but they didn't have your address at the clinic…Paris is big…You have to be careful…People like us end up getting lost.'

After the Palais de Chaillot, she turned right and we passed alongside huge buildings, which looked abandoned. I no longer knew which city I was in. It was a city whose inhabitants had just deserted it, but it didn't matter at all. I was no longer alone in the world. The road became steeper as it ran down to the Seine. I recognised Avenue

Albert-de-Mun, the garden around the aquarium and the white façade of the apartment building. She parked in front of the porte-cochère.

'You should come and see the apartment. It's on the top floor. There's a big terrace and a view over the whole of Paris.'

'And what if Solière comes back unexpectedly?'

Each time I pronounced this phantom's name, I wanted to laugh. All I had was the memory of a man in a dark coat in the police van, then in the foyer of the clinic, and in the café on the quay. Was it worth finding out more about him? I sensed that he was the same breed as my father and all his cronies I used to see long ago. You'll never know anything about those people. You'd have to consult police reports written about them, but those reports, written in such precise and clear language, all contradicted each other. What was the point? For some time, so many things had been teeming around in my poor head, and the accident had been such a big deal for me...

'Don't worry. There's no chance of him coming back now. And even if he did, he's not a nasty man, you know...'

She burst out laughing again.

'Has he lived here long?'

'I'm not sure exactly.'

She seemed to be teasing me. I pointed out that he wasn't in the phone book at the address on Avenue Albert-de-Mun.

'It's crazy,' she said, 'how much trouble you've gone to for all these details. Anyway, Solière isn't his real name. It's the name he uses for everyday life.'

'Do you know his real name?'

'Morawski.'

The name sounded familiar, but I didn't know why. Perhaps it was in my father's address book.

'Even under the name Morawski, you wouldn't find anything in the phone book. Do you think it's all that important?'

She was right. I didn't really want to look in the phone book anymore.

*

I remember that we walked along the pathways of the garden, around the aquarium. I needed to breathe the open air. Normally, I lived in a kind of controlled asphyxiation — or, rather, I'd got used to taking shallow breaths, as if I had to ration oxygen. Above all, you have to resist the panic that takes hold of you when you're afraid of suffocating. Continue to take short, even breaths and wait for the straightjacket crushing your lungs to be removed, or for it to gradually crumble of its own accord.

But that night, in the garden, I breathed deeply for the first time in a long time, since Fossombronne-la-Forêt, the period of my life I had forgotten.

We arrived in front of the aquarium. We could hardly make out the building in the half-light. I asked her if she'd ever been inside. Never.

'Well, I'll take you one of these days…'

It was a comfort to make plans. She had taken my arm and I imagined all the multicoloured fish, close to us, circling behind the glass in the darkness and silence. My leg was painful and I limped slightly. But she, too, had the graze on her forehead. I wondered towards what future we were headed. I had the impression that we had already walked together in the same place, at the same time of day, in another time. Walking along these pathways, I no longer really knew where I was. We were almost at the top of the hill. Above us, the dark mass of one of the wings of the Palais de Chaillot. Or, rather, a big hotel in a winter sports station in Engadin. I had never breathed such cold, soft air. It penetrated my lungs with velvet freshness. Yes, we must have been in the mountains, at high altitude.

'You're not cold?' she asked. 'Perhaps we could go back…'

She drew in the upturned collar of her coat. Go back where? I hesitated for a few seconds. But of course, back to the building at the end of the avenue that ran down towards the Seine. I asked if she planned on staying there long. About a month.

'And Morawski?'

'Oh, he'll be away from Paris the whole time.'

Again, the name seemed familiar. Had I heard my father say it? I thought about the fellow who had called me that day from the Hôtel Palym and whose voice was interrupted by the static on the line. Guy Roussotte. We had an office with your father, he had said. Roussotte. Morawski. He, too, had an office apparently. They all had offices.

I asked what it was that she could possibly do for this Morawski who was called Solière in everyday life. 'I want to know more. I think there's something you're hiding from me.'

She remained silent. Then she said abruptly, 'Not at

all, I've nothing to hide. Life is far simpler than you think.'

She addressed me with the familiar *tu* for the first time. She squeezed my arm and we walked alongside the aquarium building. The air was still just as cold and easy to breathe. Before crossing the avenue, I stopped on the edge of the pavement. I contemplated the car in front of the apartment building. When I came here the other night, it had looked abandoned and the avenue deserted, as if no one came this way anymore.

She said again that there was a big terrace and a view overlooking the whole of Paris. The lift climbed slowly. Her hand was resting on my shoulder and she whispered something in my ear. The timer-light went out. There was nothing above us but the glow of a night-light.

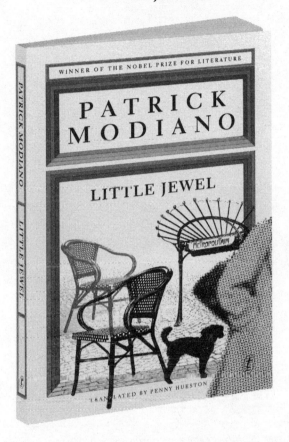